NEW YORK TIMES BEST-SELLING AUTHOR

Jake Marcionette

JUST JAKE

DOG EAT DOG

illustrated by
VICTOR RIVAS VILLA!

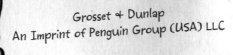

Grosset & Dunlap
An Imprint of Penguin Group (USA) LLC

I DEDICATE THIS BOOK TO . . .
NOW *THIS* IS AN EMBARRASSING TIME TO HAVE WRITER'S BLOCK!

ACKNOWLEDGMENTS: THANK YOU TO EVERYONE AT GROSSET & DUNLAP/ PENGUIN USA. ESPECIALLY KARL JONES! ALSO, BIG THANKS TO THE AMAZING VICTOR RIVAS AND MY AGENT, DAN LAZAR.

GROSSET + DUNLAP
Published by the Penguin Group
Penguin Group (USA) LLC, 375 Hudson Street, New York, New York 10014, USA

USA | Canada | UK | Ireland | Australia | New Zealand | India | South Africa | China

penguin.com
A Penguin Random House Company

ISN'T IT COOL THAT SPEECH IS FREE?

Library of Congress Cataloging-in-Publication Data is available.

ISBN 978-0-448-46693-4   10 9 8 7 6 5 4 3 2 1

CHAPTER 1
BACK ON THE BUS!

Like lots of kids, I take the bus to and from school every day. And, like most kids, I hate the bus. For me, it's a lose-lose proposition. Why? Because at Kinney Elementary, there are two different kinds of bus drivers, and they're both awful.

The worst kind of driver is the type I like to call Sergeant Sally. This one takes her job WAY too seriously: A Sergeant Sally treats her bus like it's a large yellow detention room on wheels, and she makes sure you don't forget it. On the first day of school, she already knows every kid's name. A Sergeant Sally also knows your parents'

names and has their cell numbers . . . and will call them.

You can only sit in your assigned seat on a Sergeant Sally bus. Using some kind of evil computer program, she strategically places all good friends a minimum of five seats apart.

In the past, I've been assigned to sit with a kid named Reggie, who only recited the digits of pi. Another time I had to sit with Emma, who just couldn't help herself and had to eat her sardine-and-pickle sandwich on the way to school.

It's a miracle the Sergeant Sally buses don't get into more accidents. The drivers never look where they're going. How could they? They spend all their time watching the kids.

Stand up to talk to a friend? A Sergeant Sally sees it

and calls you out by name. Toss a crumpled-up piece of paper at the kid across the aisle? Busted! Get out of your seat too soon, before the bus has made a COMPLETE stop? You've got detention, buddy.

A Sergeant Sally bus is never late. If your pickup time is 7:03 a.m., you better count on her rounding the corner and pulling up to your stop at 7:02 a.m. And she doesn't care at all if you forgot your lunch and have to run back home.

The second kind of bus driver is a Relaxed Ralph, and he seems nice enough at first.

A Relaxed Ralph always gives parents a big "good morning!" with a happy wave, but once those doors close, his bus is utter chaos. Everyone basically runs wild on Ralph's bus—even sitting in your seat is optional.

A Relaxed Ralph only knows the names of the worst kids.

He has been known to give out high-fives for perfectly thrown snowballs and well-executed atomic wedgies. He never watches his monitors. Oh yeah, and he is ALWAYS late.

This particular morning was no different. It was pouring rain as Ralph pulled into school after the second bell. Michael and I sat in the first row, knowing we'd have to sprint to homeroom to prevent another tardy.

"Have a great day at school, Joey," said Mr. Ralph #2, looking right at me as he pulled the giant handle to open the doors.

"Wow. He's getting better. Yesterday it was *Sam*. He got the *J* part right," whispered Michael as he pushed me down the incredibly steep bus stairs.

I'd say we missed the curb by about four feet that morning. Because of the rain, a raging river of disgusting brown water separated me from higher ground. Looking back at Relaxed Ralph with my best "are you kidding?" face, I saw that he couldn't care less. The bus driver was already talking on his phone.

"Go for it, Jake!" encouraged Michael. "Nothing like an early morning swim!"

With a chorus of "move!" and "jump!" and "come on!" growing behind me, I had no choice. *SPLASH!* No matter how quickly you jump back out of a puddle, you still end up with soaked sneakers.

Squishing down the empty hall on the way to class, I thought about how it was AWESOME having a best friend. Michael was a really cool kid. Once he cut his hair and stopped dressing like it was hunting season, the teachers and all the other students at Kinney Elementary stopped being so afraid of him.

Our librarian, Mrs. T., knew he was smart and encouraged him to take the placement tests for gifted classes. Michael passed easily. Over Christmas break, the school moved him into Mrs. Pilsen's class, where he joined me and the rest of the Misfits.

*NOTE: The new-and-improved Michael was all business. And NOBODY called him Wild Boy anymore. Not even me.

But change was coming to my perfect world at Kinney Elementary. Unfortunately for us, a very pregnant Mrs. Pilsen was leaving. I didn't want to say anything about her timing, BUT, a baby in the middle of the year? Hello! You are a teacher! There are young minds at work here!

We were all bummed out at losing our AWESOME teacher, but if she had to go, the Misfits were going to send her off in style. She deserved an epic good-bye party.

Of course, once we got the idea of throwing a big party, Lesley Kim jumped in and took over the whole operation. She's bossy like that, but at least she gets stuff done. With her in charge, I was confident Mrs. Pilsen would be blown away.

And I hoped she LOVED her gift! I'm sure Mrs. Pilsen never expected us to get her anything, because teaching us was gift enough! But we all chipped in some cash and got her something spectacular.

We also successfully recruited Mrs. T. as our faculty accomplice. Her job was to get Mrs. Pilsen out of the room for a few minutes while we decorated, laid out the food, and rolled out her present.

Her big surprise wasn't exactly what I would have picked out, but Lesley and all the class moms thought it was the greatest thing ever. I still can't understand the big deal. We bought her a baby stroller. Really! (I had been thinking of something more along the lines of a 3-D TV or five-tiered chocolate fountain.)

But after seeing the thing, I realized it wasn't a stroller at all. It was a high-performance baby ATV, complete with a sick aerodynamic design, monster-truck tires, and a modified suspension that guaranteed a bump-free ride. Kids these days sure are soft.

Ajit, the class brainiac and resident rapper, refused to pitch in for the stroller and insisted on writing some lyrics for Mrs. Pilsen instead. He argued that his "dope rhymes" would someday be worth way more than a stupid stroller. After he "blew up" and became a famous hip-hop star, Mrs. Pilsen could collect millions in royalties.

It would have been fine, but he demanded we all listen to him rehearse. He wanted his gift to be perfect:

YOOOO!!! Maternity is ON
because your bundle of joy.
I know I shouldn't say it,
but I hope it's a *boyyyy!*
Hoping your young gangsta
someday rocs da mic
Just like me, DJ Ajit. I bet his IQ
is out of sight.
Don't worry about nothin',
and please don't get the jitters.
Be sending you selfies and updates
straight from Twitter!
OUT!!!

8

With everything in place, the brand-new kiddie mobile parked in the middle of the class, and all of us hidden, we waited anxiously for Mrs. T. to deliver our beloved teacher.

Minutes passed, and no Mrs. Pilsen. After about a half hour of squatting behind the trash can, my legs were killing me.

Just then, an out-of-breath Mr. Yeatter came crashing into the classroom. It took a while to decode what he was saying—something about "Mrs. Pilsen" and "baby" and "labor" and "hospital"—but it soon became clear our teacher wasn't coming back. APPARENTLY, the soon-to-be most important person in the WORLD decided to show up early, and our teacher was rushed to the hospital.

After eating a few slices of pizza and guzzling a can of Coke, Mr. Yeatter started checking out Mrs. Pilsen's tricked-out baby stroller.

"Hey kids, what's that?" asked Mr. Yeatter as he circled around the carriage.

"That's our gift to Mrs. Pilsen. It's an ultra baby wagon," said Lesley proudly.

"Sweet! Mind if I take it for a spin?" Mr. Yeatter said, half kidding, as he rocked it back and forth, impressed with its fine craftsmanship and sturdy build.

Without hesitation, Lesley skillfully kicked off the wheel brakes and swiftly pushed the gift into our coat closet for safekeeping.

Not a chance, BUDDY! Step away from the stroller.

10

CHAPTER 2
THANKS, STUPID BABY!

Soon a whole bunch of teachers started showing up in our class. They all tried to act concerned about us and wanted to "check in" and see how we were doing. But, interestingly, the more "concerned" teachers popped by, the more our party food disappeared. Vultures!

Eventually, Mrs. T. returned to school. She was the one who drove Mrs. Pilsen to the hospital. Wow, Mrs. T., you took your job of keeping Mrs. Pilsen busy a little too seriously.

Mrs. T. let us know that Mrs. Pilsen was doing fine and that she was REALLY sorry about missing the rest of the school year and had promised to send us updates every day.

Sorry? Mrs. Pilsen didn't have to be sorry. She didn't do anything wrong. The only one that needed to be sorry was that baby for coming a week early. He owed us all a big-time apology!

That night at dinner I told my parents what happened, and I ended up getting yelled at by my mom. In retelling the story, I referred to the newest Pilsen family member as "that stupid baby" and my mom freaked out.

"You CAN'T call a baby 'stupid,' Jake!" roared my mom.

"Why not? He knew what he was doing. Couldn't he let his mom be the center of attention for a minute while we said good-bye?" I said. "But you're right, Mom. He

isn't stupid. That baby's a spoiled JERK!"

Mom got even more upset. It looked like Little Lord Pampered Pants could do no wrong. After dinner I found myself clearing the table AND washing the dishes. Thanks, kid!

Maybe I would ask all my classmates to pitch in money for a second gift for Mrs. Pilsen! Hey, Mr. Saggy Diaper . . . how'd you like to wake up from nappy time and find a brand-new, floppy-eared, supercute beagle puppy sitting on Mommy's lap? That's competition you don't want, son!

No good-bye party. No cake. No ice cream. No nothing! All we got was a spoonful of disappointment followed by a heaping helping of angry crazy!

The school had struggled with budget cuts and was in a tight spot to find a long-term replacement. Their answer was Ms. Cane.

Her first day at school was something I'll never forget. With Principal McCracken standing by her side, Ms. Cane warmly greeted each of us as we entered the class. She was all smiles, hugs, and laughter.

Um, her physical appearance was, how do I say . . . different. Let's start with her hair color: pink!

Not just light pink, or a touch of rosy pink, but over-the-top CRAZY pink. Like cotton-candy pink. It looked like there was an Easter egg on her head.

And then there were the tattoos. Lots of people I know have tattoos. My uncle Dave has a bunch, and some teachers in school have them here and there. No big deal. But Ms. Cane had gone overboard. She made no attempt at being discreet. Who has a picture of a parakeet tattooed to their neck? Ms. Cane did. And then there was her convict-style knuckle tat that read LOVE PETS.

After a few minutes of laughs and stories and "so nice to see all of your bright, shiny faces" stuff, Principal McCracken had heard what she needed to hear. Looking overwhelmed as usual, she wished the new substitute teacher the best of luck and headed back to her office.

That's when everything changed. I swear to you, as soon as Principal McCracken had left the room, Ms. Cane crept over to the door and popped her head into the hall, just to make sure McCracken was long gone. So sneaky!

Chucking her grimy backpack on the desk, Ms. Cane started to unload her personal junk: books . . . coffee

mugs . . . and pictures. Wow! Ms.
Cane was an animal freak!

Soon her desk was covered with
pictures of "her babies." There was a
menacing-looking Rottweiler named
Boomerang, a turtle named Mr.
Fred, and a colorful parrot named . . .
wait for it . . . Lil' Cane!

"Okay!" said Ms. Cane. "A bit more
about me—and this is important, so
pay attention—I've been teaching
for twenty
years. Before
that, I was a prison
guard at Maryland Super Max.
But that job got too boring.
You can say I'm kind of an
adrenaline junkie. I wanted the
ultimate challenge: a job that

'SUP.

tested the limits of my mental toughness and perseverance. I found it—kids!" Ms. Cane said, smiling.

From sweet, loving Mrs. Pilsen to an animal-obsessed, tattooed former prison guard in twenty-four hours. I was already planning my trip to PETCO to price puppies. It is ON, Mr. Baby!

"Like I said, I have twenty years on the job, and this is my last assignment before retirement. In three months, I am OUTTA here!

"This brings me to my main point. And don't be shocked by this because I am brutally honest," said Ms. Cane. "I like kids just fine, but I don't really want to be here. I didn't want this job, but, because I am a team player, I agreed to babysit you nerds until the end of the year," said Ms. Cane.

Wow! That was unexpected. I loved her brutally honest AWESOMENESS!

"I realize Mrs. Pilsner was a great teacher," said Ms. Cane. "I have no interest in trying to replace her, or follow her curriculum or continue with anything she was teaching.

"Like I said, I'm in full-blown retirement mode, and since I've worked in the district so long they're not about to fire me. Unless of course I do something REALLY insane!" said Ms. Cane as she laughed uncontrollably. Everyone immediately felt uncomfortable.

Michael and I looked at each other, not believing what we were hearing. It went from bad to OH MY GOD in a matter of seconds.

"Please don't think this is a bad thing . . . we can have a good time! I see lots of reading, watching movies, and maybe even some arts and crafts in your future," said Ms. Cane. "But . . . I don't want any problems.

"So, let's establish some ground rules. We can call these 'Ms. Cane's Do's and Don'ts.'"

Grabbing the chalk, Ms. Cane headed for the blackboard.

"If followed to the letter, these simple rules will guarantee classroom harmony and prevent any of you from spending the last three months of school in detention."

#1. DO BE ON TIME, RESPECTFUL, CALM, AND QUIET. OUR CLASSROOM SHOULD APPEAR TO BE A SANCTUARY OF LEARNING.

#2. DO NOT ASK ME ANY QUESTIONS. DIRECT ALL YOUR QUESTIONS TO THE QUESTION ROCK.

Ms. Cane reached into her bag and took out a big gray rock with the words QUESTION ROCK inscribed in bold black letters. She placed it on a desk in the back corner of the room.

"At your age, you

already know the answers to ninety-nine percent of the questions you would ask. You just don't realize it," stressed Ms. Cane. "If you need reassurance that badly, just ask the Question Rock. It will help you become more confident and develop critical-thinking skills. Trust me!"

"What about the one percent of questions we DON'T already know the answers to?" asked the class clown, Banderson. (Ohhhh . . . kill 'em!)

Banderson's real name was Ben Anderson. He played the trumpet in the band and was a super-funny kid. So we nicknamed him Banderson.

"That sounded like a question to me. Haven't you been paying attention?" asked Ms. Cane. "Mr. Funny . . . go and speak to the rock."

Ms. Cane pointed to the Question Rock and waited until Banderson sheepishly got up and walked to the back of the class.

#3. DO ADDRESS ME ONLY AS MS. CANE.

"I am an educated and independent woman," advised Ms. Cane. "Ms. Cane is how you will address me."

#4. DO NOT SPEAK ABOUT THIS CLASS OUTSIDE OF THIS CLASS.

"This one is simple. What happens in this class stays in class," said Ms. Cane.

Wow again! I didn't know we were going to school in Las Vegas! Just like the commercials. Was this legal?

"I want our time together to be easy. I don't need headaches. And I certainly don't need your parents sticking their noses in my business," explained Ms. Cane. "If you are cool with me, I'll be cool with you."

Not knowing what to do, Banderson started to slowly shuffle his way back to his desk.

Smiling and giggling to the rest of the class, he almost made it . . .

"Did you find your answer, Mr. Funny?" asked Ms. Cane, breaking the uncomfortable silence.

"Y-Y-Yes?" stammered Banderson.

"Great! Please share it with the rest of the class," requested Ms. Cane.

"Ummm . . . Don't even ask you the one percent of the questions we don't know the answers to?" said Banderson.

"That sounds about right! I told you the Question

Rock would work. Thank you, Mr. Funny, for proving my point," said Ms. Cane.

Typically, when we have a substitute, the kids in my class will push the envelope and take advantage of the situation. We'll switch seats, pretend to be someone else, talk, text, and generally goof off.

That morning, there was NONE of that. You could hear a pin drop, and every kid sat at the straightest of attention. All eyes were forward. There was a new sheriff in town, and her name was Ms. Cane.

Thankfully it was Friday. Michael was sleeping over that night, and we had a lot to talk about.

CHAPTER 3
ROGER THAT

Man, I was nervous! Sweat rolled down my back, and I started to breathe heavily. The pitch-darkness and eerie silence provided little comfort. From a distance, we could hear the lonesome cries of a chained hound.

It was a damp, humid night. Outside, light rain pattered on the driveway, making it difficult to hear footsteps. It wasn't my first mission, but the old nerves started to get the best of me. Was I ready? Did we have all the right gear? We'd rehearsed and planned for weeks knowing there was no room for error. I didn't know why, but I doubted myself.

Maybe because that time it was personal.

My night-vision goggles were snug, and the foamy end of a radio headset hung inches away from my mouth. Something wasn't right. What had I forgotten? Ignoring my strict instructions, I broke radio silence.

"*Ninja 44*. This is *LeBron6*. Equipment check. Over."

"Roger that, *LeBron6*. Solid copy. We are a GO. Maintain radio silence. Out."

"Negative, *Ninja44*. Need to double-check on the N-Strike Elite Hail-Fire blaster. All clips ready and operational? Over."

"Are you kidding, Jake? Sorry, I mean, Roger that, *LeBron6*. I'm all set. We got this. Relax! OUT!"

Michael was an ice cube. Cool under pressure with no worries. His confidence may have been his own worst enemy.

I'd been to this rodeo before. Many times! And always came away empty-handed. Sometimes severely bruised. Our target that night was deadly, and she was scheduled to arrive home at 8:00 p.m. It would be dark outside, and all the lights in the house would be off. The perfect ambush. Michael took up his position at the top of the stairs, while I was strategically hidden behind the couch. GOTCHA!

Michael decided to go with the Nerf N-Strike Elite Hail-Fire blaster that held an astounding eight clips with a 144-dart capacity. If his semi-auto barrage of darts didn't finish off the target, I was there for reinforcements.

My weapon of choice was the Nerf Blazin' Bow Blaster.

Call me old school, but I loved the feel of real bow action at my fingertips. It made hunting Alexis considerably more challenging. But just in case that failed me, I also had a Nerf Vortex Vigilon holstered to my leg. Poor girl, she didn't know what was about to hit her.

Suddenly, headlights illuminated the dark house. A minivan loaded with girls pulled into the drive. Hearing a familiar voice and the obligatory "Thank you Mrs. So-and-So," I knew it was go time.

"Ninja44. This is *LeBron6*. Target approaching hot zone. Over."

"Roger that, *LeBron6*. I have a visual. Scanning with thermals. Over."

"Solid copy, *Ninja44*. Lock and load. Let's do this!"
Hoo-ah!

Alexis bound up the front steps singing the same sound that only moments before had been blaring out of the van full of middle-school girls. Obviously practice had gone well.

Fumbling for keys, she dropped her oversize backpack. *Thud!*

Seconds later the dead bolt clicked and the door slowly swung on its hinges. With my night-vision goggles, I could see Alexis standing in the foyer trying to find the light switch. It was my idea to tape over it. Awkward darkness would provide the cover we needed to attack.

But as soon as she felt the tape, Alexis knew it was a trap. To her credit, she didn't panic. Alexis quickly backed against the wall and then became motionless. She was thinking.

I knew Michael didn't have a clear shot. The banister was in the way. Alexis was supposed to be standing directly under the light fixture, but she wasn't cooperating.

My radio softly crackled with Michael's voice.

"*LeBron6.* I have visual but no real shot. Permission to throw the Nerf football. Over."

"Negative, *Ninja44.* NEGATIVE! ROE prohibits firing upon enemy in close proximity to Mom's expensive lamp. Just wait. She'll move. Over."

Before I could hear Michael's reply, my world lit up like a solar flare. Somehow Alexis had worked the switch free from the tape and flicked on the lights. Blinded by the incredible brightness, we ripped off our night-vision goggles and opened fire.

Michael laid down a semi-auto barrage of Nerf darts, and I followed with a flurry of Nerf arrows. After launching all ten of my spongy missiles, confused and still semi-blind, I reached for my side arm. But the iron grip of death grabbed me by the wrist.

"Nice try!" snarled Alexis as she flung me to the ground and jumped on my back. Before I knew it, I was begging for mercy. Alexis had me in her famous cross-face chickenwing hold. She also had my gun and my headset. Not again!

"Hello, Michael," whispered Alexis in the microphone. "I have your comrade. You're next. If you lay down your blaster, I promise not to embarrass you as well."

"Don't do it, Michael. She's LYING!" I shouted, only to have my arm thrust closer to the back of my neck.

Michael wasn't an idiot. If Alexis captured us both, all future sleepovers would be forever ruined. We couldn't live with the shame!

"Hold your fire. I'm coming out," announced Michael. Walking down the stairs, Michael held his gigantic Nerf blaster above his head. I could see Michael standing safely behind the railing, considering his options.

"That's far enough, Wild Boy. Now kick your gun over to the door, and I'll let little Jakey go so you two big boys can continue your tea party," Alexis said with a laugh.

"Okay, okay. Relax," said Michael as his gun slid across the wood floor and banged against the door.

"MORON!" screamed Alexis, hopping to her feet, ready to blast Michael. But what she saw stopped her dead in her tracks.

Looking like a pro quarterback ready to throw the winning touchdown, Michael stared down Alexis with my multicolored Nerf football. In our game of make-believe Nerf war, Michael was holding a nuclear weapon. You don't want to get hit with that thing. First, it really hurts. Second, since it had rained all week, the ball was waterlogged. Things would get very messy upon impact.

Alexis seethed with anger. But she wouldn't surrender. Immediately she started spraying Michael with Nerf darts. As fast as she could pull the trigger, Nerf projectiles popped out of the blaster. But she wasn't hitting him.

Slowly walking forward, Michael sidestepped, weaved, ducked, pivoted, and jumped out of the way of Alexis's full clip of darts. Apparently, years of Tang Soo Do training had useful benefits.

Quick and agile, Michael was impossible to hit. In an

instant, he was standing directly in front of an out-of-ammo and frustrated Alexis.

"Drop it! Or I will whip this at your head," said Michael.

"Dude! Hit her NOW! Don't wait," I yelled, getting to my feet and begging Michael to blow up Alexis with two pounds of wet, Nerfy destruction.

Instinctively grabbing me as a human shield, Alexis held me close, trying to defend herself from a sloppy Nerf ball to the head.

Michael faked her out and went for a side shot. Alexis, sensing danger, decided to abandon her position and shoved me into Michael's line of fire. This brief instance of confusion was all she needed to escape into the hall bathroom.

With my dear sister locking herself inside, we had her exactly where we wanted her: unarmed, trapped, and ready to be taunted.

"Yes! Captured at last. How's that feel, Alexis?!" I

shouted through the door as I high-fived Michael. "Boo-yah! Don't worry, I'm recording this glorious moment."

Taking out my cell phone, I wanted video of Alexis emerging defeated and angry.

We had done it. Me and my best bro had defeated the previously undefeated world champion of Nerf war.

Just goes to show you what detailed planning, determination, and teamwork can achieve in life. While we stood victorious and gloating, I heard a distinct and confusing sound.

Was Alexis's cell phone powering on? I could hear the unmistakable weird space music of her phone. Then she switched to speaker and made a call. *Ring, ring, ring . . .*

"Hi, Mom!" said Alexis in her sweet-angel voice.

"Hi, sweetheart. Where are you? Is practice over?" asked Mom.

"Yeah," Alexis said sadly. "It's over, but jerk Jake and his creepy friend Michael locked me out of the house. It's so cold and rainy outside. Can you open the door?"

I could only imagine the thoughts that instantly ran through my mom's head: pneumonia, stranger danger, wild animals!

"They did what?!" screamed my mom. "Honey, I'll be right down."

Suddenly, the whole house started to rumble. Our old wood floors creaked as Mom sprinted to the rescue. She wasn't going to be happy seeing us upstairs amid the aftermath of our Nerf battle. Michael and I were supposed to be in the basement watching basketball. Not good!

"Retreat! Basement, now!" I screamed as we ran toward the stairs. Within seconds, we were once again stretched out on the couch with two giant bowls of popcorn. *Nothing to see here!*

CHAPTER 4
THE NATURAL

Yeah, of course my mom was annoyed by our attack on Alexis. But since Michael was sleeping over, she couldn't get that mad. My parents loved Michael. He was all "yes, sir" and "no, ma'am" when they were around.

I didn't worry too much about Mom or the Heat vs. Celtics game I was supposed to be watching. Lacrosse tryouts were next week and I was panicking. Pacing around the basement, cradling my stick wildly, I was trying to practice my lax moves.

On the unfinished side of our basement, we have a lacrosse goal and netting. It's where I practice shooting in the winter. But without a goalie, I can't tell if I'm getting better.

"Michael, pause the game for a minute. I need your help," I said.

"What? You know I don't know how to play lacrosse," said Michael.

"The fact that you grew up in Maryland and know nothing about lacrosse is crazy. Don't worry, I don't want to throw and catch with you," I said. "Just stand in the goal and try to stop my shots."

"No thanks!" said Michael.

"Come on, man! I have all the equipment. Helmet, chest protector, pads, goalie stick . . . everything. Don't be a wimp," I said. "I'll even use a tennis ball. Don't worry, you won't get hurt!"

Michael knew I wouldn't stop. With a heavy sigh he got off the couch and put on all the goalie gear.

After a few easy warm-up throws, he was all set.

"I don't expect you to stop any," I said reassuringly. "But this is super helpful. Just stand there and try to look like you know what you're doing."

"Yeah, yeah, yeah . . . come on. Let's get this over with," said Michael, clearly annoyed at having to get up from the comfy couch.

I started him off with a few easy low shots. After the first couple bounced past him, Michael's inner competitor awoke. He made a quick adjustment to the way he was holding the stick, moved forward, bent his knees, and before I knew it, he started making some saves.

"Wow. This is pretty cool. Easier than I thought," said Michael.

"You're good, man! Do you want me to start trying now?" I said sarcastically.

"Sure. Go ahead," said Michael.

"Okay. Your wish is my command. But don't get mad!" I said.

Rolling to my left, I ripped a sidearm shot as hard as I could. Sure, it was a jerk move, but he had all the protective equipment.

Lucky for Michael, I missed the goal completely. But he didn't seem to mind.

"Sorry! That wasn't cool. I shouldn't have done that. I'll slow them down," I said.

"Why? Was that fast?" asked Michael innocently enough.

"Kind of a hard shot, yeah," I said. "You didn't think so? You're okay with that speed?"

"Sure. Do it again. But this time, can you give me a chance to save it?" asked Michael.

I couldn't tell if he was being a wise guy or not.

Backing up to the opposite wall, I grabbed another tennis ball and cranked an overhand blast, aiming at the top corner of the goal.

Michael instantly shifted his weight to the left, moved his feet slightly, and lifted the head of the goalie stick to block the shot. *WHAT!?*

Okay. Beginner's luck. Scooping up another ball, I fired again. Getting off a low rocket, Michael effortlessly kicked the ball to the side. By this time, he was really into it.

After about ten minutes, it became clear that Michael was some kind of natural lacrosse-goalie freak. He had all the qualities required for the position: quickness, lightning reflexes, no fear, and a high threshold for pain.

"You've NEVER played before? Ever?" I asked.

"No. Never. I swear! This is really fun, though," he said. "Come on, Jake, shoot some more!"

We soon forgot all about the basketball game. At some point during our practice, Dad came downstairs to check in on us. I didn't know how long he'd been watching, but after one of Michael's more spectacular saves, Dad had seen enough.

"Break time, you two," said Dad from his darkened corner of the basement.

"Hey, Dad, you have to see this," I said. "Michael is unbelievable!"

"I know. I saw. Michael! Wow! You're incredible. Do you think you'd like to play lacrosse this season?" asked my dad.

It didn't take much convincing to get Michael interested in playing. I had all the equipment he needed, and Dad suggested we go to the lacrosse fields in the morning.

"You guys look thirsty. How about a drink and a snack?" said Dad.

"Yes, sir!" said Michael. I nodded in agreement.

As Dad headed upstairs to get us our treats, I figured I'd give the impossible a try.

"Hey, Dad. How about a couple Pucker-Up Ice Lemonades and a few Galactic Brownies?" I asked.

"That's funny!" My father laughed as he continued walking up the stairs. Even he wasn't brave enough to do that.

Those were Alexis's special "after-workout" treats. She bought them with her own money, and I wasn't even allowed to look at them.

"Don't worry, Dad. I'll ask Alexis," I said.

Running upstairs, I saw her in the kitchen with Mom.

"Hey, Alexis. You don't mind if Michael and I have some of your special snacks, do you?" I asked.

"Yes, I mind. And NO, you cannot," answered Alexis matter-of-factly.

"Oh. Okay. I understand. Still upset about being captured in the bathroom? Don't worry. Happens to the best of us. You're getting old. Slowing down. First Nerf wars . . . then maybe . . . I don't know . . . lacrosse?" I said.

"Hilarious. The day you two little kiddies are better than me in lacrosse is the day I retire!" said Alexis.

"Really? You wouldn't have to quit. Just give us two

41

Pucker-Up Ice Lemonades and two Galactic Brownies. That would do nicely," I said.

"What are you talking about? You stink at lacrosse, and Wild Boy breaks boards with his head. You guys have a long way to go before you're in my universe," said Alexis proudly.

"You're right. Michael isn't a big lacrosse player like you. But, I bet you can't score on him," I said.

"Michael? A goalie? Anytime. ANYWHERE!" crowed Alexis.

"Great! Right now . . . downstairs! You get one shot from the far wall. If he makes the save, it's SNACK TIME!" I screamed, pointing my finger dangerously close to my sister's face.

My attempt to anger her was successful. She immediately went to her room to retrieve "Tiger." That's the name of her game stick. Much like her drinks and brownies, no one was allowed to look at Tiger. He only came out for special occasions.

I told Michael to put the gear back on, and both my parents came downstairs to watch. Alexis smiled smugly as she saw Michael standing in the goal. She felt at home in the basement.

We had everything down there because of Alexis. She set up the whole thing and literally would spend all day in our cellar shooting, playing wall ball, and honing her game. She even saved her babysitting money and bought a radar gun to clock the speed of her shots. Let's just say she shoots REALLY hard!

When I asked if she wanted to first warm up a bit, maybe get a few practice shots, she just rolled her eyes. Okay. Suit yourself.

"Remember, you only get one step off the back wall before you have to shoot. I don't want you running in too close to Michael—that wouldn't be fair," I said.

Alexis said nothing. She knew the rules and just kept throwing the tennis ball into the air, waiting for Michael to give the "ready" sign.

Michael looked all set and light on his feet. But just as Alexis started to bring back her stick, Michael stepped out of the goal and took off his helmet.

"Sorry, Alexis, I just want to check one thing. I'm not a big fan of the Pucker-Up Ice Lemonade. Do you have any Kiwi Strawberry?" asked Michael.

Alexis's death stare was intimidating. She didn't like waiting, and now Michael was trying to be funny. She gripped her stick extra tight. *Here comes the ATOMIC!*

Michael got back into the goal and nodded it was okay. With a mighty scream, Alexis unleashed a blistering, canon-like blast toward the top-right corner. She had practiced that shot a thousand times. And knew with certainty it was going to hit its target.

The only thing she didn't count on was Michael's insane goalie abilities.

Before the ball even left the stick, Michael was already moving to the right spot to make the save. With the oversize head of the goalie stick swung across his body,

Michael effortlessly gobbled up Alexis's shot and calmly rolled the ball back to her.

Alexis was the only one shocked by what happened. She just stood there and stared at her beloved Tiger in disbelief. As it turned out, Alexis didn't have any Kiwi Strawberry.

But Michael decided to enjoy a Pucker-Up Ice Lemonade anyway. Why not? He earned it.

Good Guys 2-Alexis 0.

CHAPTER 5
WHO DID IT?

As soon as Monday morning rolled around, it was back to school and Ms. Cane. Michael and I sat on the bus dreading our new reality.

The Question Rock? Was she kidding? What if I had to go to the bathroom? Should I just leave and not ask permission? So confused.

"By the way, thanks a lot for telling me how 'great' and 'AWESOME' the advanced class was," said Michael sarcastically. "I definitely felt safer in Mr. Yeatter's class."

As soon as I walked into class, I knew something was wrong. Ms. Cane was standing in front and she looked angry. Well, I mean, angrier than usual.

"So, guess who got called down to the principal's office on Friday after school?" Ms. Cane asked the class. "I did. Apparently, one of you complained to Mom and Dad about the rules in this class," said Ms. Cane. "Are you guys kidding me? We had a deal! You don't bother me, and I won't bother you."

Walking from the front to the back of the room, Ms. Cane slowly scanned the class, thinking aloud: "Now, I want to know who did it. Which one of you ruined it for all of us?"

Coming closer and closer, it didn't appear she had a prime suspect in mind. Which was good, considering I suddenly remembered an innocent dinner conversation the week before with my mom. Not sure, but I MIGHT have mentioned the whole "no homework" arrangement in Ms. Cane's class.

Since Mom was a hovering helicopter parent with Principal McCracken on speed dial, I knew immediately who called. My mom was the snitch. And I was about to get called out.

"Right now, I want to hear from that person. I'd like a sincere confession. This is the court of Ms. Cane, and I am the judge and jury," the pacing teacher said with a sneer.

Ms. Cane was staring at each kid individually. Looking, analyzing, and searching for any sign of guilt. Once she passed my desk, I thought I was in the clear. But she suddenly turned around and headed back in my direction.

"We'll sit here all day. I WILL find out who you are!" announced Ms. Cane as she locked in on me. *Gulp!*

But she wasn't dealing with some rookie. I knew I had to stay cool and quickly decided to go with my standard confused face: tilted head, squinted eyes, serious nose scrunch. I wasn't about to confess anything.

Besides, there was NO WAY Principal McCracken would ever tell Crazy Pants anything about my mom. BFFs don't do those sorts of things. Nice try, lady. Who'd she think she was dealing with?

Tapping her finger on my desk, Ms. Cane stood in front of me. It looked like she was about to say something when a highly agitated and practically hysterical Dudley Malone leaped out of his seat screaming and crying.

"It was me . . . It was me . . . IT WAS MEEEEEEEEEEEE!!" Dud shouted with tears streaming down his face. "My father called yesterday. I begged him not to, but he wouldn't listen.

"I told him how great you are!!!" moaned Dudley as he rolled on the floor between desks. "I'm sorry—I never thought my dad cared so much!"

Dudley spent the rest of the day sitting in Ms. Cane's wooden chair of self-reflection. OUCH! It was a torturous contraption with no cushion, and it looked like it belonged in a grandma's living room. Would it have killed her to get a rocker?

The rest of us were hit with an avalanche of class work.

The only happy kid was Ajit. He was beaming with delight and kept yelling "Yeah, *boyyyyy!*" every time Ms. Cane handed out a new assignment.

Underneath Ajit's pretend "gangsta" exterior was a true geek. All the hip-hop clothes and gold chains still couldn't hide his inner nerd. It REALLY didn't help that he rapped about geometry:

My name is Ajit, and I love quadratic equations.

Mess with me, son,

and you'll be covered with abrasions.

I'm a super-duper math star reppin' *B'more, yo!*

You think that triangle's obtuse?

Lord have mercy, you gots to go!

So go get your TI-84 plus, your apps,

and your momma;

I do this stuff in my head, boy,
like a math-boss Dalai Lama!

Considering he was already doing high-school calculus, Ajit made quick work of the grade-level math questions. As fast as Ms. Cane handed them out, he turned them back complete and perfect.

"It looks like you are quite the smarty, Mr. Jaokar," said Ms. Cane, who was clearly annoyed by our resident math whiz.

"Thank you very much, Ms. Cane. Yes, math does come easy to me. Perhaps you have something more challenging?" asked a cocky Ajit.

"I am SO glad you asked. I do have something *very* challenging for you," said Ms. Cane.

"Ajit, see that dry-erase board in the corner? One careless classmate mistakenly drew on it with a permanent Sharpie. The custodian said it's ruined and can never be cleaned. I don't believe that," said Ms. Cane as she dropped a roll of paper towels and a spray bottle on Ajit's desk.

"I want you to prove him wrong, Mr. Jaokar!" encouraged Ms. Cane as she helped Ajit to his feet and gently nudged him in the direction of the board.

Not the challenge MC Ajit was counting on. He wanted to say something so bad but caught himself just in time.

Ajit was too smart to make it worse. Lesson learned—be careful what you ask for in Ms. Cane's class. Too funny!

CHAPTER 6
FRIENDS AND FAMILY

During that first week of Ms. Cane's rule, it was so hard not to tell my parents everything that was going on: no real class work to speak of and NO homework, ever. Ms. Cane apparently didn't believe in it.

Having dodged a bullet with my mom's first phone call, there was no need to aggravate the academic police. *Nothing to see here, officer. Everything is fantastic. I'm learning so much!*

Instead, I skillfully directed the nightly dinner conversation to my latest obsession: conquering Facebook and Twitter. Sure, both of these are nothing more than online popularity contests . . . BUT . . . for some reason, they were contests I desperately wanted to win!

I don't think I was insecure or desperate for attention—it was just the competitor in me. And I especially wanted to crush my sister, Alexis, in this contest.

Although she is probably the meanest person on the planet, for some completely unexplainable reason, she has loads of friends. And I had to find a way to get more friends and followers than her, without resorting to fear-based tactics.

For years she's been secretly intimidated by my AWESOMENESS. I was self-confident; I didn't need to go to the mall surrounded by ten "yes-kids" I barely knew. Gossiping about my "friends" wasn't the limit of my human interaction.

Though my popularity had blown up earlier in the year when everyone fell in love with my Kid Cards, those glory days were far behind me. That rocket ship to fame and fortune came crashing back to earth after Bo Wilson ruined it for everyone.

It turned out Bo was too immature to express his true love for Katie Whipshaw. Instead of calling her up, asking her to a dance, or passing her a note, he decided to create a highly unflattering Kid Card of her. Makes perfect sense to make fun of the girl you supposedly like, right?! Principal McCracken immediately put an end to all Kid Card activities.

Thoroughly enjoying Mom's pasta that evening, I discussed my strategies for social-media domination. As usual, my dad couldn't help but interrupt.

"Technology!? That's what's wrong with kids today. All plugged into your Blue Teeth i-Tablet, Cloudy-Thingy. Just happy lambs going to the intellectual slaughterhouse. Not me! I still read the paper and love a good book. My business is built on REAL personal relationships . . . face-to-face . . . mano a mano! I don't live my life behind a computer screen. That doesn't prepare you for the real world. When I was a kid, we played outside! Do you even know what tree bark feels like?"

I had to admit, I didn't. But I was curious as to why he thought it mattered. I could just read about tree bark online.

"So, Jake, why do you want so many 'friends'? What's the big deal?" asked Alexis, pretending not to be too interested.

"Why? Because everyone knows that once you hit one hundred thousand friends, you automatically win a brand-new Lamborghini," I said matter-of-factly. "I just hope they still have a yellow one in stock when I get there."

"WHAT! Are you kidding me?!!!" screamed Alexis.

Gotcha.

Those were Alexis's weaknesses—a shiny yellow LAMBO and being WAY too gullible. Everyone knows five thousand friends is Facebook's maximum allowance. Besides, who gives away super-expensive sports cars?

From reading her browser history, I knew Alexis spent hours online looking at Lamborghini pictures, reading about the cars, how much they cost, and the celebrities who drove them.

I bet she imagined her and her goofy friends cruising around with the top down and acting too cool for school. Of course, they'd be wearing oversize sunglasses and carrying those tiny annoying dogs in their purses.

"No, genius! Do you really think they give away free cars?" I asked.

"I knew that . . . jerk!" shouted Alexis.

"But seriously, it's just fun. You get to meet a lot of kids you'd never have the chance to know," I said.

"Meet? You don't 'meet' anyone," said my dad.

"That's enough," said my mom calmly as she turned her

focus on me. "But, sweetheart, having so many friends and followers puts a lot of pressure on you to maintain those relationships. Right?"

Uh-oh! DANGER! DANGER! Mom's academic success protection system detected a disturbance in Sector Nine. She was about to unleash the hounds and destroy all potential threats and distractions.

"Not at all! Basically, my network does the work for me," I said.

"What do you mean?" asked Alexis, not so innocently.

Alexis and Mom both stared at me and waited for an answer.

I had nothing to hide. It's not like Alexis could use any of my strategies, anyway. Without good content, the system doesn't work. And by good content, I mean *funny* content. Alexis was a lot of things . . . aggressive, selfish, intimidating, slimy, manipulative, quick to anger (I could go on and on) . . . but funny, she wasn't.

"It's easy. All you have to be is funny. If you can make

your readers R-O-F-L you'll get tons of friend requests, group invites, retweets, and followers," I explained to Alexis. "Your problem is, sorry to say, you post boring girl stuff! Boring!" I said, pulling out my phone and looking at some of Alexis's recent tweets.

Alexis Mathews @AlexisMathews99 · Oct 15
Hey y'all! At the mall with my BFF's. Who knew sushi and green tea smoothies were so DELISH!

Alexis Mathews @AlexisMathews99 · Oct 15
Just chillin. Does anyone want to come over and play DanceDance?

TWEET?

Alexis Mathews @AlexisMathews99 · Oct 15
Teen Wolf season finale tonight! Can't wait. #SoPumped

Alexis Mathews @AlexisMathews99 · Oct 15
I hate my uneven tan lines. UGH! Lax girl problems!

I explained in detail how my swelling numbers of friends and followers was basically built by posting the most hilarious thing I'd found that day!

Awkward photo of a teacher with funny Instagrammed thought bubble? It went up. Epic-fail video of some skateboarder from Australia? Bam! On the wall. Little kid nailing his father in the crotch with a bat? I'm all over it!

With each post and tweet, I always included language sure to capture the attention of any kid audience: *OMG WEG, SOOO CUTEEEE, or GOTs to Retweet This!* The more the content got seen and heard, the more people tuned in.

#CanYourDogDoThis

GET A TURTLE TODAY!

A little immature, maybe . . . but what do you expect? I'm in sixth grade! Unsophisticated? Just giving the people what they want! Effective? I had already put together 490 friends and 3,900 followers . . . enough said. And I was just getting started.

CHAPTER 7
B-BOY!

Even though my sixth-grade year had been turned upside down by the arrival of Ms. Cane, I was still dialed into my upcoming lacrosse tryout. Michael and I practiced all the time. On the weekends, my dad would take us to the park so we could train on the turf field.

Michael got better every time we worked out. Of course, my game was already supertight. But having Michael in goal allowed me to take my shooting to the next level. We were both ready to match our skills against the best kids in our county for a spot on one of the highly selective Cobra travel teams. I was confident the A team was in my future.

On the day of the tryouts, the weather was perfect. There were loads of kids from Kinney Elementary there. Unfortunately for me, I got put into an evaluation group with Jason the Jerk and a couple of his dopey friends. They all had flowing long hair, crazy multicolored shorts, and started almost every sentence with "bro."

"Hey there, little nerdy guy," said Jason as he patted me on my helmet. "You must be confused, Jake. The Squirts tryout was yesterday!" That got a huge laugh from his buddies.

"No, Jason, I'm in the right place. But if you want to talk about being confused, let me ask

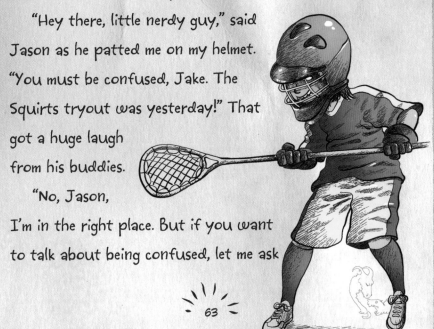

you this: What's two plus two equal?" I said.

It took a few seconds for Jason to get the joke. But once he figured it out, I received a swift punch to the face mask, which sent me flying. Luckily, I was wearing my helmet and had on all my pads.

Of course, Jason still hated me because of the whole Michael "fight" thing earlier in the year. If I'd known at the time he was one of the area's best lacrosse players, I probably would have handled the whole situation differently. But I hadn't, and now I had to deal with it.

Trying to get to my feet, I acted cool and laughed off Jason's surprise punch. But I was a little wobbly. After making it up to one knee, somebody grabbed me by the arm and yanked me away from Jason. It was Michael.

"WHAT!!!! No way! Wild boys don't play goalie. They run around the woods hunting deer with their bare hands. Let's see how tough you are now!" mocked Jason as he smashed his gloves together and jumped up and down, super psyched at his chance for payback. Although he

wouldn't dare act that way in
school, Jason knew the lacrosse
field was his domain.

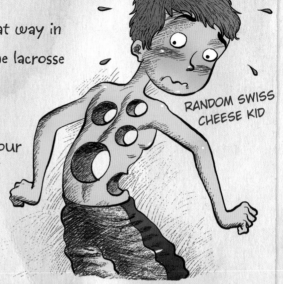

RANDOM SWISS
CHEESE KID

"I'm going to make
Swiss cheese out of your
body, Michael. You
better get ready for
a whole lot of pain
today," said Jason.

Keeping his cool, Michael ignored Jason, and
we walked away and began to warm up. Soon the coach
blew the whistle and the tryouts began.

— — — — — — — — — — — —

At the end of the tryout, I thought I had played
AWESOMELY! My shot was on, I scored a few goals in
the scrimmage, and I walked out of there certain I was
A-team material.

I also heard from a few kids that Michael had played
surprisingly well, so I was hopeful he made the B team. At

least we'd be practicing on the same night, which was great.

When I received my "Welcome to the B team" email two days later, I was devastated. I spent that night reviewing the entire tryout in my head, trying to figure out what had gone wrong.

I texted Michael and told him my bad news. But at least there was a chance we'd be on the same B team. It was a slim chance, but since he'd been training with ME, I thought he had a shot.

Just found out I didn't make A. CYBT?! At least there's the possibility we be ballin' on the same team. I hope we're B brothers in arms!

He didn't text back right away. Usually, he zips off a funny message instantly.

Five minutes passed, and still nothing. Ten, twenty, thirty minutes went by, until finally I heard the familiar buzz.

Oh man! That's messed up. Sorry to hear that Jake. You're not going to believe it . . . I made the A team. Now, I'm not that excited.

Michael made the A team and I *didn't*?! For a few minutes I thought it was some kind of bad dream. Splashing water into my face, I tried to wake up from that nightmare. Nope. It was all real.

When I told my dad, he couldn't believe it. Not that I made the B team, but he couldn't believe Michael made A. And man, was he excited. He asked me if it was okay if he called Michael to congratulate him. I said no.

The next day at school all anyone wanted to talk

about was the new goalie phenom. He was an overnight celebrity in lacrosse-obsessed Howard County. I even noticed his Twitter account had blown up with lacrosse fan girls and all the guys from the A team. Even kids from other teams were following him now.

A kid who never picked up a stick makes the A team on one of the state's most competitive travel clubs. That's the stuff they make movies about. And all I wanted to do was feel sorry for myself.

Heading to my locker, I knew he'd be waiting for me. As soon as I saw Michael, I felt like the world's worst friend. I wanted to turn around and sulk back into the crowd of kids.

All I could say was "great job" as we walked in silence to class. I still wasn't ready to talk about it.

That morning the class was extra quiet. I gave Michael a "what the . . . ?" look when I saw the word SILENCE! printed across the dry-erase board.

Miraculously, Ajit had been able to clean the board.

Having learned his lesson, he was now taking his sweet time with all his assignments. Most of the day, Ajit just played games on his phone. His inner nerd had been broken like a wild stallion.

"Hey, Banderson, what's going on?" I asked.

That was greeted by a group *SHHHHHH!!* from the rest of the class. At the bottom of the board, in smaller print, it read: ABSOLUTELY NO TALKING TODAY.

After sitting there and doing nothing for what seemed like hours, without even a word from our new teacher, I was done. I didn't make the A team, and I was in no mood to be ignored. Unlike Ajit, my inner nerd could never be tamed.

CHAPTER 8
NAME GAME

Maybe it was my inherent proclivity for the pursuit of erudition that compelled me aloft. (SAT-prep alert! Never too early to start.)

Without fear, I got up and approached our big, bad substitute. Enough was enough. Sure, no homework and a teacher who didn't care sounded good in theory. But I was only in sixth grade! The lacrosse scholarship wasn't looking so good, and I had a LOT I wanted to do in my life—and a lot I needed to learn!

Ms. Cane was too locked in on her computer to notice me standing there. What I saw almost made me laugh. She was on Facebook? Seriously?! Updating her profile, while I stood there waiting to be taught . . .

But it wasn't her profile she was looking at. It was the fan page for Dog Groomers R Us. The admin panel was open, and she was just sitting there, staring at the screen. Weird.

"Darn computer!" muttered Ms. Cane as she pushed her laptop. "From bad to worse. What do YOU want?"

A VERY ACCURATE REENACTMENT.

"You know you can reposition that image so the dog's head isn't chopped off," I said, pointing at the headless pooch on the screen.

"What do you know about Facebook?" asked Ms. Cane, quickly changing her tone.

"Tons! I've got almost four thousand followers and counting!" I bragged.

A smiling Ms. Cane slowly reached over her desk and grabbed a chair. She playfully patted the seat and motioned for me to join her.

Over the next few hours, I learned a lot about our pink-haired sub. It seemed she was more scared than mean. Apparently, because of the bad economy, Ms. Cane wasn't going to receive all the retirement money she had planned on.

That meant she had to find another job to help pay the bills. And because of her love for animals, Ms. Cane thought launching a mobile dog-grooming business was a good idea. That's what Dog Groomers R Us was all about.

When she was in the middle of searching for a grooming

truck and setting up her business, the school reassigned her to teach our class. That's why she wasn't teaching. Ms. Cane was too busy trying to secure her own future. I decided to give Ms. Cane a little advice. *Way to go, Mrs. Pilsen's selfish baby. Is there no end to the chaos you've created?*

"Dog Groomers R Us? That's the name you came up with? Are you sure about that?" I asked.

"What do you mean? What's wrong with the name?" asked Ms. Cane.

"Nothing's wrong with it. It's just boring," I said. "I get the whole Toys 'R' Us thing but . . . Where's the swag? It's not very inspiring."

"I think it's catchy. People are going to LOVE it. I love it," insisted Ms. Cane.

"And that's the problem. It's your idea, so of course you love it," I said with a smile. "Let's see what they think?" I said, pointing to the rest of the class. "We have a lot of smart kids. If the name is great, why not put it to a vote?"

Pushing out from behind her desk, Ms. Cane looked alive and energized.

"Good idea! I love kids, AND I know they are going to love it," said Ms. Cane.

She "loves" kids? She has a funny way of showing it . . .

Calling for attention, Ms. Cane quickly outlined her future plans for the entire class. It was the first time she had spoken to us directly in days.

Nobody knew what to make of her sudden change of character. Was it a trap? Did she have a secret stash of dry-erase boards that needed scrubbing? After a long, awkward pause, Banderson slowly raised his hand.

"Permission to speak?" requested Banderson.

"Permission granted," said a smiling Ms. Cane.

Shaking his head in utter disbelief, Banderson looked around at the rest of the kids before he spoke.

"You want us to help you?" asked Banderson.

Ms. Cane said, "Yes. Let's forget the rules for now."

Everyone looked at one another, trying to figure out

what to do. Soon they were all nodding in agreement and the class collectively decided a fresh start was the way to go.

A giddy Ms. Cane swiftly approached the board and wiped it clean. In big bold letters she wrote: DOG GROOMERS R US.

Turning to the class, Ms. Cane waited for reactions.

Kinney's sixth-grade enrichment class studied the board and thoughtfully considered the name. Some took notes, others opened their phones, and a few whispered in small groups.

Banderson was the first to raise his hand.

"Are you the only dog groomer in your business?" he asked.

"Yup. Just me. I'll do all the grooming and washing," answered Ms. Cane.

"In that case, you're lying," stated Banderson.

Ms. Cane didn't understand.

"The US part!" explained Banderson. "As in *more than one groomer*. It's false advertising!"

"Good point, Banderson," I said, taking over the role of official moderator.

"Is dog grooming the only thing you do?" asked Lesley Kim. "What about cat grooming?"

"I'll start with just dog grooming. But, what the heck, cats need to be washed, too," said an eager Ms. Cane.

"In that case, change the name to Cat-and-Dog Groomers R Us," said Lesley.

"I see your point," said Ms. Cane, who looked more dejected by the minute.

"What about llamas?" asked Raffi Lyons.

ADORBS.

Raffi was a crazy llama lover! His family ran a llama farm, and it was the only thing he talked about.

"Sounds good. I'm open to anything. Besides, llamas and alpacas are so adorable," gushed Ms. Cane.

"Did you just say *alpaca*? Well, let me tell you something Ms. Cane. *Al-PUKE-as* stink! Try getting an *Al-PUKE-a* to pull your wagon," Raffi said with a laugh. "And forget trimming their toenails. They'll spit all over you. Don't be fooled. They're not the cuddly little fur balls everyone thinks they are."

"Raffi . . . my man! Great stuff. Solid contribution, bro," I said, walking over and guiding him back to his seat, trying to avoid a full-blown llama-rific meltdown.

"I think we all agree the name's not great," I said. "But . . . can we come up with a better one for Ms. Cane?"

My classmates loved the challenge. Quickly, the rules were established, and everyone got five minutes to think of their best name.

Being a creative guy, the challenge should have been no

problem for me. But I had nothing! The best I could come up with was Suds and Growls. Luckily, the rest of the kids did better. Here are the finalists . . .

PAMPERED POOCHES

MAD CLEAN WASHIN' MACHINE

THE WAGGIN' WAGON

NEVER LET 'EM SEE YOU SHED

MS. CANE'S HOUSE OF HORRORS*
(THANK YOU, BANDERSON.)

PET SCAM-BULANCE** (ANOTHER
BANDERSON.)

SHINY AND NEWTS

THE FUR MOBILE

TWO BROKE GROOMERS

DOGGIE DAY-SPA

After reading the names, we all agreed there wasn't a clear winner. Nothing really stood out as AWESOME. With everyone thinking out loud and frantically trying to come up with a killer name, Michael stepped to the front of the class.

"Fur Cuttery, Inc.," announced Michael calmly. He really sold it by following it up with the very convincing tagline "We deliver!"

Everyone nodded and smiled.

"We have a winner!" yelled Ms. Cane.

Was I the only one who knew his mom worked at Hair Cuttery? Not too creative.

CHAPTER 9
DEAR PARENTS

Ms. Cane was psyched about the new name for her business.
But she soon got way more than she bargained for.

Like dangling a scrap of red meat in front of a pack
of hungry wolves, the intellectually starved sixth-graders
became very aggressive.

"Excuse me, Ms. Cane, did you buy your truck yet?" asked Mitch Leone.

"No, not yet. Probably in a few weeks," said Ms. Cane.

"Are you going for a hitched trailer or a van/truck conversion?" asked Mitch.

"I don't know. What's the difference?" asked Ms. Cane.

"A lot! What about onboard power? Are you thinking a propane or diesel generator? Yamaha or Honda?" questioned Mitch.

A confused-looking Ms. Cane now faced a sea of raised hands. "Wow, so many great questions. It looks like I really need to do some homework," said Ms. Cane.

Ms. Cane truly had homework-a-phobia! She hated to give homework and obviously couldn't do her own.

"How much are you going to charge? Are you going to be all cash? Will you take credit cards?" asked Lesley.

Lesley's parents owned a yogurt shop in town, and she helped out on the weekends. Every time I'd see her working I'd try to get her attention. But it never worked.

Even if she saw me, free yogurt was NEVER on the menu. CHEAPO!

Ms. Cane was frazzled and tried to calm the students. But the questions kept flying!

"Do you have a cool logo?"

"Are you going to need pet insurance?"

"Okay . . . okay . . . let's settle down. Looks like ole Ms. Cane needs to go back to the drawing board. Thanks for your input. Now, for the rest of class, please have some fun and relax," said Ms. Cane.

Ms. Cane sat at her desk in disbelief. She had SOOOO much to do. Then it hit her. Sitting right in front of her was the answer—a whole bunch of go-getting brainiacs.

Feverishly typing on her computer, Ms. Cane quickly cranked out a take-home permission slip and passed copies out to the class. After reading it, I had to laugh:

NO FREE YOGURT FOR YOU, JAKE.

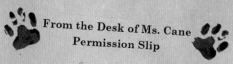

From the Desk of Ms. Cane
Permission Slip

Dear Parents,

My name is Ms. Cane, and I have the exquisite good fortune of being your child's ubstitute teacher for the remainder of the school year.

This year's standardized tests are already taken. With Mrs. Pilsen on unexpected ave—unreachable as per doctor's orders—I would like to suggest a radical and fun eparture from the "average" curriculum. As you all are aware, your children are r from average. They are extraordinary! Thusly, I want to challenge their creativity d hopefully spark a passion for future success through entrepreneurship.

With your support, I am proposing a class project whereby all the children rticipate in the planning and operation of a small business. At this point, I am king for your input as to which of the following opportunities are best suited for r gifted young learners:

OPTIONS: Please select one
- ☐ Pet-grooming business
- ☐ Medical-waste recycling initiative
- ☐ Highway bottle-and-can-collection cooperative
- ☐ Cell-phone tower monitoring and maintenance program

I understand this unparalleled real-life internship might not appeal to all of you. at is the case, please let me know, and accommodations can be made to place your in Mr. Yeatter's standard class.

Regards,
Ms. Cane

_____   _____
Student Name   Parent Signature

lease check one:
- ⊐ Can participate in once-in-a-lifetime gifted-class internship
- ⊐ Please place in standard sixth-grade class

ive a kid a boring curriculum, and maybe they'll graduate from high school. each a kid a skill and how to start a business, and he or she will have a job ter college! ~ Ancient Chinese Philosopher

Ms. Cane would have all the parents in the palm of her hand. Even I was impressed with her craftiness. *Ancient Chinese philosopher?* LOVE IT!

The last potential roadblock to Ms. Cane's master plan was Principal McCracken. Ms. Cane needed her okay on the whole crazy idea.

As soon as Ms. Cane handed out the permissions slips, she rocketed out the door and headed for the main office. With the promise of happy parents (i.e., no more phone calls) and the suggestion of a possible National Blue Ribbon School award, Principal McCracken was no match for the devious Ms. Cane.

Strolling back into class, Ms. Cane thought her future employees needed some last-minute encouragement.

"Kids! I'd like you all to go home tonight and get those permission slips signed. This is going to be an incredible adventure. You know, real-world experiences," urged Ms. Cane. "This is the kind of stuff Ivy League colleges love!"

Ajit could hardly contain his excitement. He tried to

high-five himself!

"But even if your parents don't want you to participate, you're in luck! Mr. Yeatter's class is about to start a five-part series on the evolution of woodwind instruments. Fun! Right? I hear he's actually bringing in an oboe."

I had no words. I was in the presence of a MASTER.

CHAPTER 10
GAMER EYE

At my house, dinnertime was our opportunity to come together as a family. My parents always loved to hear about our days. For me, that was easy. Being a fine, law-abiding citizen, I never had much to worry about. For Alexis, it was a different story.

Alexis HATED dinnertime. The nightly experience drove her crazy. She loved food but dreaded the price she had to pay to get it. And that price was answering my parents' questions.

Mom: So, sweetie, how was your day?

Alexis: Fine . . . (munch, munch, munch)

Dad: Just "fine"? You'll have to do better than that.

Alexis: Okay . . . it was *great* . . . (munch, munch, munch)

Mom: Really? Really?!

Alexis: *heavy sigh* I had some classes, ate lunch, and came home. Oh yeah! I need twenty bucks for spirit week.

Dad: How'd you do on the history exam?

Alexis: Why?

Dad: Because I'm your father and I want to know how you're doing.

Alexis: I'll tell you for half your burger. . . .

Dad: Done!

Typically, Alexis could withhold information long enough to eat half of everyone else's plate. I never understood what the problem was with her. It's not like they were asking to read her diary. For that, all they had to do was come to me!

That night I jumped right in without being asked. I had the biggest news ever!

"You'll never guess what happened today," I said, very excited about my announcement.

"Wild Boy finally figured out how annoying you are and beat the crap out of you?" answered Alexis.

"ALEXIS!!! Please. Of course Michael wouldn't do that," said Mom.

"Funny! But no, the best thing ever happened. My class is starting an advanced-level internship project. We are going to spend the rest of the year launching and operating a pet-grooming business," I said proudly.

"Outstanding! Enough with math you'll never use and reading about ancient dead guys walking around in tablecloths. Some work experience is what you need," said Dad.

"But wait a minute, hon, before we get all crazy. Does this mean there are no more real classes?" asked Mom. "No math, science, history?"

"Yup. Since we already took our state tests, Ms. Cane wants to try something different. Show us kids how the real world operates. Right, Dad!" I said.

"NO! NO! NO! ARE YOU KIDDING ME!" screamed Alexis as she stood up with her knife and fork gripped tightly. "I have to go to school, take notes, study, get tested, and worry about grades while Jake plays with dogs all day?"

"We have to wash them first," I said, winking at her. "But seriously, it's going to be tough. First, we have to plan and research the industry. After that, we'll break into groups that are responsible for marketing, accounting, and operations," I said, trying to sound all serious and mature.

"What part of the business are you working on?" asked Mom, calming down enough to catch her breath.

"Me? I want to be in charge of marketing the business. I figure with my online expertise and ability to connect with millions through social media, I'm the right guy to put the world on notice about our AWESOME new pet business."

Dad's face quickly went from "amazing news" to "jeez." Maybe I should have kept quiet?

"Really, Jake? Don't you think you should try something new? What about accounting?" said Dad.

Keenly sensing the shift in the dinner atmosphere, Alexis quickly sat down and collected herself.

"You guys sure are lucky. But . . . I think Dad is right. How often do you get a chance like this to try something outside your comfort zone?

"Besides—and I don't want this to sound like I'm trying to GET you, but I am concerned—you spend way too much time online," said Alexis in her most caring voice.

"And I only say this because of what I saw on the Dr. Oz show yesterday," said Alexis, looking over at my mom.

Mom was a Dr. Oz FANATIC. If that guy said some weird nut from the Panamanian rain forest could make you healthier, guess who instantly turned into a Central American squirrel monkey?

"What did he say?!" shrieked mom in a frantic tone.

"He did a whole special on teen addictions. And guess what's number one?" asked Alexis.

"Drama!" yelled my dad, knowing exactly what she was up to.

"Shhhhh! Be quiet. What? What's number one?" pleaded my mom.

"The INTERNET! I'm not an expert, but based on the signs he mentioned, I think Jake could be

EAT YOUR DINNER, JAKE. DON'T FORGET THE WEIRD NUT.

addicted," said Alexis.

"Oh my god! The INTERNET!" said Mom, turning to my dad for support.

"He has all the symptoms. Look at the way he always leans forward over his meal. Too much time tapping on his iPad. Dr. Oz calls that 'social hunch,' and it can permanently curve his spine," said Alexis.

"WHAT!" shrieked Mom.

"Have you also noticed Jake squints a lot?" said Alexis.

91

"Dr. Oz calls that 'gamer eye.' He'll need glasses soon for sure!"

"Jake, be honest, do you have gamer eye?" asked Mom.

Before I could answer, Alexis delivered a knockout blow.

"And I REALLY didn't want to bring this up . . . but, he's gotten really soft and puffy. Dr. Oz says the Internet and teen obesity walk hand-in-hand," said Alexis as she sat back, smiling.

"My man, I have noticed you've put on a few pounds," said Dad. "Maybe you should take a break from the whole 'online' thing for a while."

"Jake. If Dr. Oz says you're a hunched, visually

impaired, obese teen, then YOU NEED TO LISTEN!" pleaded my mom.

"I heard gamer eye is serious business," said Dad.

Dinner had taken a drastic turn for the worse. Suddenly, I was taking fire from all directions.

What to do? Thinking. Pondering. I needed a way out. The whole time, Alexis sat across from me, grinning. She waited for my next move.

And then it came to me. The path forward was clear but wouldn't be without casualties. I just stared at Alexis knowing what I was about to do would change our relationship forever.

CHAPTER 11
SLEEPOVER

"And I agree with Dr. Oz 1000 percent. I've definitely been spending WAY too much time online," I said. My mom looked happier already, and was clutching my dad's hand. *Easy does it, Mom, your baby boy is going to be okay.*

Seeing an opening, I skillfully switched the focus of the conversation to Alexis.

"However—and I'm not trying to *get* anyone, but I do want to share with you my concerns—I've discovered something that troubles me deeply," I said.

Alexis had that stupid look on her face. I'd seen it a thousand times. She was trying to figure out what was coming. *Too late!*

"Alexis, I don't want you to screw up your life. But your friends and your recent stunts are worrying me. You want to go to a good college, right?" I asked.

TOO BAD. SO SAD.

"Of course I do," replied Alexis, now looking stupider by the second.

"And that's why I'm scared. I'm afraid you'll end up in juvie," I said, trying desperately to shed a tear. No luck.

"JUVIE! What are you talking about!" demanded my dad.

"I'm talking about lying, stealing, and serious criminal behavior. That's what I'm talking about, Dad!"

"Jake, just because you're addicted to the Internet, a B-team lacrosse player, and have thousands of fake online 'friends' doesn't mean you can make up stories about me," said Alexis.

"I'm not addicted to the Internet. But I do see a lot of funny stuff online. Unfortunately, it's not very funny when it involves your sister," I said. "By the way, how was that 'sleepover' last Saturday at Shelby's house? Vandalizing the neighborhood at two in the morning must have been totes cool!" I said.

ALEXIS'S "SLEEPOVER"

Alexis denied everything. I was "a liar out to get her." According to her, the girls stayed in the basement watching movies and braiding one another's hair.

Alexis kept her cool while explaining her story, knowing the slightest hint of emotion would signal guilt. She also knew the damaging Vine video I saw posted on Shelby's Twitter page had been deleted.

Unfortunately, for technology-challenged Alexis (obviously she got Dad's genes), what she hadn't counted on was the ease with which Vine videos can be copied and saved. Click . . . copy . . . paste . . . BUSTED!

Reaching for my phone, I had the damaging Vine vid up and running within seconds. We were all treated to a smiling and laughing Alexis hurling toilet paper all over Arnold Bernardi's house. The video was time stamped 2:04 a.m. Not very smart, Shelby!

"Wow, Alexis! You should play softball!" I said, admiring the height and distance of each roll.

Alexis was out of her chair and on me quicker than I'd anticipated.

Man! Her speed-and-agility classes were really paying off.

She had a CRAZY look in her eyes. Alexis tried to rip the phone out of my hand. But I resisted, feebly holding the fragile device over my head. Suddenly, I felt the phone snatched from my grasp.

"I'll take that," said Dad. He just stared at both of us in disgust.

After hours of tears, crying, sobbing, and promises of "I'll never do it again," Alexis's fate was decided—no more sleepovers! *Ouch! That's going to leave a mark.*

To a thirteen-year-old girl, taking away sleepovers is like taking the car keys away from a senior in high school. It kills them socially. They miss out on all the unsupervised fun. And they basically have nothing to gossip about the following week in school.

I didn't see Alexis the rest of that night, though I could hear her weeping down the hall. *Better watch my back,* I thought. I might have gone too far. That night, I kept both eyes WIDE open!

CHAPTER 12
GET A JOB

Ms. Cane gazed over her class of enthusiastic workers. She nodded confidently, recognizing her own genius. With a hardy "Let's. Do. This!" we all were off and running into the wild world of entrepreneurship.

As the first order of business, our pink-haired leader assigned positions within the company. She proudly rolled out the dry-erase board Ajit had so successfully cleaned. On it was this pyramid-like diagram of boxes with wacky titles like Pooch Wrangler, Sudsing Sensei, and Customer-Service Jedi assigned to each. She called it the Org Chart or the Big OC.

The OC would become the epicenter of our classroom and the business. Where your name appeared on the OC was HUGE! It determined your grade, the quality of your classroom life, and whether or not you could be bossed around. The farther down you were, the worse it was. Everyone wanted to be on top.

"As you all can see, I've only assigned one position so far," stated Ms. Cane. "Michael, front and center.

"It gives me great pleasure to introduce Michael as the CE-YO of Fur Cuttery, Inc. He came up with the name, he's a natural leader, and I know he has the right stuff to lead us to success," said Ms. Cane.

Michael stood in front of us, blushing and smiling.

Arghhhh!!! Yeah, he came up with an unoriginal name and a predictable tagline. That made him the big cheese? Michael-mania was getting annoying.

"The rest of you are encouraged to interview for any other position on the OC," said Ms. Cane. "Please take a minute and decide which one you want. If you have any questions about the job titles, just ask. I came up with some wild names just to keep it *ballin'* up in here," said Ms. Cane, trying to sound cool.

"After we've heard from everyone, Michael and I will make the final decisions," announced Ms. Cane.

Interesting! Michael better not forget who trained and mentored him on the lacrosse field. He owed me big-time.

I quickly located the job I wanted. Ms. Cane was calling the head of marketing the Boss of Buzz. Perfect. If she wanted to create sick hype and buzz for Fur Cuttery, Jake Ali Mathews was her guy.

Sitting down, waiting for my turn to interview, I noticed DW III pacing in the back of the room. He was practicing what looked like a speech. And he somehow had changed into a jacket and tie.

Where did that come from? I had to admit, he looked VERY professional.

"What's with the outfit?" I asked.

"Outfit? Very humorous, Jake. Boys don't wear *outfits*, we dress for success," scoffed DW III.

"What position are you going for?" I asked.

"What else? Boss of Buzz, of course!" said Donald. "Since Wild Boy somehow snagged the chief executive position, it's the only other job worth having."

"You might want to consider something else. The Boss of Buzz is going to be me, for sure," I asserted confidently.

"Really? Where's your résumé? Do you have any experience? Professional references?

Can I see YOUR marketing plan?" Donald asked.

"No! Who has any of that stuff?" I asked mockingly.

Unfortunately for me, he did!

DW III might have been a rich jerk, but he was a prepared rich jerk. Pulling out a really cool leather briefcase, he showed me his perfectly typed documents. That kid was GAME ON, and I was still sitting on the bench.

"Jake . . . relax. Once I'm the real BOSS, I won't forget you. You can be my assistant. Just remember, I like my hot chocolate with extra low-fat organic foam and those really tiny marshmallows," said DW III.

Oh well, at least my dad will be excited when they put me in accounting.

When it was DW III's turn, he picked up his briefcase, straightened his tie, and marched right over to Ms. Cane and Michael. The kid was confident. DW III immediately shook their hands firmly and presented his business card! I did NOT see that coming. But before DW III could say anything, Ms. Cane hit him with a direct question.

VAIL

"Do you own any pets?" asked Ms. Cane.

"Yes. We have a teacup Maltese named Vail, and Father has a Pomeranian named Maybach.

MAYBACH

They're adorable!! Very well behaved," answered DW III.

"Do you take care of them? You know, wash them, brush out their coats, brush their teeth, trim their nails?" asked Ms. Cane.

(OR AN EWOK FROM STAR WARS . . .)

"Of course! Our dogs are very well groomed," assured DW III.

"No, no . . . do YOU take care of them?" asked Ms. Cane, pointing to DW III.

"Me? Gosh, no! Our housekeeper, Mrs. Kingston, is in charge of all that," said DW III.

"Thank you, Donald. Next!" shouted Ms. Cane.

"Wait. Wait! Don't you want to read over my plans?" asked DW III as he scrambled to hand Ms. Cane a fully tabbed color-coordinated binder.

"Donald. Thank you. We'll let you know," said Michael as he stood up and "guided" DW III back to his seat.

A proud Ms. Cane fist-bumped Michael as DW III returned to his chair.

"So, Jake, let me guess? Boss of Buzz?" asked Ms. Cane.

I smiled and gave a meek double thumbs-up.

"Before I let you say something stupid like Mr. Wall Street over there," said Ms. Cane, motioning to DW III, "the job is yours. Just don't screw it up."

Remaining silent, I stood up, nodded in appreciation, and got out of there as fast as I could. For once I said nothing and accepted my well-deserved reward.

Ajit was named Grandmaster Cash and was in charge

of accounting. Made sense. Being a math whiz, Ajit was the smart choice to keep track of the money.

Lesley Kim was selected Queen of Clean, and she was in charge of operations, which meant the grooming of the animals and cleaning of the truck.

At the end of the morning, the OC was filled out, and we were ready to get going.

I would be lying if I didn't admit to being EXTRA happy at seeing Naomi Sinclair placed in the "Beehive," which was what the marketing department was called. Get it? Bees? Buzz?

Ahhhh! NAOMI SINCLAIR! Her name sounded like a really expensive dessert Mom would buy in the frozen-food section! Or a celebrity perfume.

Blond, perfectly straight hair, blue eyes, and oversize round nerd glasses. She was the real deal!

She also refused about ten of my friend requests. And she didn't follow me back on Twitter, either.

Over time it became clear to me that she was doing the old hard-to-get routine. Since I started school back in September, I'd only spoken to her once. It was an encounter I'd rather forget.

One day coming out the boys' room, Naomi stopped me in the hall and told me I had toilet paper stuck to my shoe. All her friends made horrified faces, shrieked "EWWWWW," and pointed at me. Naomi bent down and freed me from my embarrassing shackle of shame.

Maybe I grossed her out, but no worries! That was all about to change. I was the Boss of Buzz!

CHAPTER 13
UP AND RUNNING

It didn't take long for Fur Cuttery, Inc., to come alive.

Little did any of us know, Ms. Cane had already bought her truck. It was one crazy pet mobile with cutting tables, an oversize sink with shower attachment, and a vacuum/hair-dryer system.

Ms. Cane gave us the grand tour and demonstrated all the cool features. It had that new-pet-grooming-truck smell.

But once the tour was over, the atmosphere quickly changed. Lesley Kim swiftly asserted her authority as Queen of Clean. Handing out buckets, mops, sponges, soap, and gloves, she ordered the maintenance associates back to the truck for some heavy-duty scrubbing. DW III, who was on her team, shot me a look of pure DISGUST!

Now the real pressure was on me. I was the Boss of Buzz. And Fur Cuttery, Inc., and I needed to find some four-legged customers.

Being a man of action, I had my new marketing team assemble in the back of the classroom. All the kids had their cell phones and there were several computers we could use. Perfect. The marketing team was ready to roll.

Within minutes the Fur Cuttery, Inc., Facebook page was up and its Twitter account was open. I blasted my network with links, posts, and some initial retweets just to get the Fur Cuttery buzz rolling.

Blake created a funny paw-print logo for the company, and Tanner met with Ajit and Lesley to figure out exactly what services we offered pet owners and how much we charged.

After an hour, the marketing team had all the preliminary stuff nailed down and it was GO TIME.

I decided to keep it real simple. Each member of my team had to call their parents, grandparents, neighbors, cousins, teammates, and anyone they knew who owned a filthy dog or cat.

Whatever they had to do: beg, plead, annoy, harass, bother. We needed that first customer.

As that first morning turned into lunchtime, we still didn't have any customers. For some reason, my mom wasn't picking up her phone. She would have been an easy sale. I didn't even try to call my dad. I knew he wouldn't do it, especially since we didn't own any pets.

Ms. Cane kept coming over and poking her head into our "office" (an area in the back of the room made up of old blankets and jump ropes). *Geez! Rome wasn't built in a day, Ms. Cane. Chillax!*

Returning from lunch, I tried to avoid making eye contact with Ms. Cane. She'd be looking for good news, and I didn't have any to give.

I hadn't taken three steps into class before I heard her booming voice.

"How's it going, Jake?" asked Ms. Cane.

I thought about ignoring her and making a run for my blanketed hideaway. *Better not. She'd just come looking for me.*

"Oh hi, Ms. Cane. How's it going? Not great!" I said. "Lunch was awful."

"What? NO! Marketing. . . . What's going on with promoting the business, Boss of Buzz? I borrowed a lot of money from the folks over at RV Junction for that ultra-cool grooming van. We need to start getting some action real soon," said Ms. Cane.

"Oh yeah! Sorry. Umm . . . it's going okay. But it's still early, we've been making calls, but so far, nothing," I said.

"Look, I am counting on you. Does everyone on your team have their sales pitches memorized?" asked Ms. Cane. "What kind of quota did you give them?"

Pitch? Quota? What? I didn't know if that was code for some secret prison language, but I was thoroughly confused.

"The script has to be tight, and they all need to be reading off the same page," said Ms. Cane.

I just sat there nodding in agreement, pretending to know what she was talking about. I was in big trouble.

"Before I forget: Here's a great tip. You're leading a team. BUT, just so you know, sooner or later, someone on your team is going to test your authority," said Ms. Cane, springing to her feet like she was ready to rumble.

"When they do, you need to be ready. At Maryland Super Max, when things got a little tense, I'd spark up my stun gun. The crackle of 50,000 volts turned fierce lions into little bitty lambs." Ms. Cane laughed as she fondly reminisced about the good ole days.

"OF COURSE!!! . . . You can't do that. But, you'll need to carry your own kind of 'attitude adjuster' to keep the inmates in check," said Ms. Cane.

"Remember, Jake, you and your team are setting the stage for the success of Fur Cuttery, Inc. Break a leg!" encouraged Ms. Cane as she shoved me off back in the direction of the Marketing Department.

WOW! I didn't know if I was supposed beat up everyone on my team or rehearse for some kind of school play. The rest of the day I just faked it and tried to ignore the fact that we didn't get one customer.

CHAPTER 14
FEAR GAME

"DINNER!!!" called Mom.

Yes! About time. I was starving—I didn't get that late-afternoon snack I needed. AWESOMENESS doesn't happen on an empty stomach.

Sprinting downstairs, I saw Alexis already sitting at the table. Ever since I was forced to reveal the secrets of her sleepovers, Alexis had gone into complete shutdown mode. Not one word had been spoken between us.

Apparently, my brotherly duties had wide, far-reaching consequences. Once my parents learned of the late-night lawlessness, they contacted the parents of ALL the girls involved. Let's just say it was going to be a while before their next hair-braiding party.

Since Mom and Dad knew they weren't going to get anything out of my sister the mute, they looked to me for their daily school update.

MUTE SISTER!

"How's business at Furry Cuts?" asked Dad.

"That's FUR CUTTERY, Inc., *Daaad*," I responded.

"Exactly! So how is it going?" asked Dad.

"Fantastic. I got the website up, and our Twitter and Facebook are launched," I said.

"I'm *so* proud of you, Jake!" gushed Mom. "Or should I call you 'Mr. Boss'?"

"That does have a certain ring to it, Mom," I said, rocking back in proud reflection. "But my title does come with a lot of pressure. We need customers, and I'm feeling the heat," I said.

"Michael's being tough on you, huh! Good for him. An incredible athlete and an effective leader—that boy has a VERY bright future," said Dad.

"NO! Not Michael. Ms. Cane! Michael doesn't do anything except sit around and trade Snapchats with his new lax bros. I'm the real brains of the operation," I said.

"Oh yeah, and she started getting all intense with me. Asking about my team's 'script' and how much was their quotey or something like that," I ranted. "I have NO idea what she means."

My dad started laughing. He spent the next ten minutes explaining exactly what Ms. Cane was talking about. As if I'm supposed to know all this adult, real-world stuff.

Evidently, big companies do exactly the same thing I did. They put a bunch of workers in a room filled with phones and each employee has to call random people and try to sell as much junk as possible.

The Big Guy also explained that a *quota* is the exact amount of calls or sales each worker has to make each day. Managers have to be tough enforcing these requirements to make sure the workers keep annoying people all day long.

"My suggestion is that you write out a little script about the company and tell your team how many calls they need to make each day. Your goal should be to have everyone repeating the same company message," suggested my dad.

"Yes, Jake, work together with your team and you'll do great," said Mom.

"With a daily quota, you'll soon discover who the slackers are and which team members you'll need to fire!" said Dad.

"Really, honey? Is that what you want to teach your son?" asked Mom. "Jake, there is nothing wrong with being a nice boss."

Dad shot Mom a look of disgust. He only knew one way, and it CERTAINLY had nothing to do with being nice. Dad didn't believe in smiley faces, gold stars, or participation trophies. He only respected hard work and results. I think Dad would really like Ms. Cane. Maybe she could join his bowling team.

THE DUDE

"Okay, Jake. Pop quiz! You're a general in the army, leading a team of soldiers into battle. Would you rather be feared or respected by your troops?" asked Dad.

"I don't know? Am I going to win? Do we have enough food? I need to know the exact scenario," I said.

"It doesn't matter!" yelled my dad. "You're at WAR, son, and you need your soldiers to perform. So which is it? Fear or respect?"

I was stumped. I had no idea which was better. How about NONE OF THE ABOVE? Because it really didn't matter, anyway. Whatever I said would be wrong. And then, being wrong, I'd have to hear the lecture. There was always a lecture from "teachable moment" Dad.

I decided not to play his game and sat there in silence. Suddenly, the tension was broken.

"FEARED!" answered Alexis.

So she speaks after all!

"Very good, sweetheart. You're correct," answered Dad.

WHAT! So THIS time there was a right answer. Not fair. I was about to say "FEARED!"

"You see, Jake, even if you are respected, those around you, even a family member, might still decide to stab you in the back," said Alexis as she coldly looked right through me.

"It's better to be feared. I learned that the hard way. Sorry, but can I be excused?" asked Alexis as she got up to leave the table. "Obviously, I need to go and work on my fear game."

We weren't used to seeing Alexis walk calmly away from the dinner table. No fork tossing, no thrown-down napkin? Everyone was a little shocked by her lack of explosiveness.

"Good night, Alexis! Have fun with your 'fear' homework. Don't worry, though—I already think you're terrifying!" I laughed. "I fear you'll show up at my house twenty years from now and want to live on my couch. I fear your bad breath after you devour a plate of tacos. I also FEAR for the little kids in the neighborhood when you get your driver's license!" I yelled.

Mom gave me the "enough" look. *Time to shut it down.*

Yet another fun night at the Mathews' dinner table. Who knew what Alexis the Terrible was cooking up for me? But I didn't have time for her attempt at intimidation. I had a team to run and customers to find.

CHAPTER 15
CAT/DOG

"What the heck's a QUOTA?" asked Banderson.

"It means you need to try harder," I answered.

I quickly explained to the team they were each now required to make at least twenty calls a day. But before they got started, we had to review the new script I had written that morning.

Fur Cuttery, Inc., Call Center Script:

(Make Sure You Are Nice!)

Dial . . . Ring . . . Ring . . . Call Answered.

Victim: Hello!

121

You: Good morning/afternoon/evening, my name is XYZ. How are you on this glorious day/night? (Wait for answer.) By the way, do you have fleas?! (Wait for outrage . . . NOW, hit them with the funny!) KIDDING!! I meant to say: Does your dog or cat have fleas? A matted coat? Stinky breath? Gross toenails? If so, I have your answer—FUR CUTTERY, INC.! We're a pet-grooming business 100 percent run by kids from Kinney Elementary School. Sounds great, right? (CLOSE THE DEAL) So, what time would you like us to come over and groom your cat/dog?

"I don't like it," said Tanner Scales. "Why would I say 'Good morning/afternoon/evening'? And I don't think too many

people own cat/dogs these days? I'm pretty sure they are extinct."

Tanner was immediately reassigned to a different task, and I moved Naomi Sinclair into the call center. She seemed to get it right away. Soon all the Customer Service Jedi were off and running, bothering whoever they could think of.

That morning I set up the company's Yelp and Google Review accounts, which soon would be filled with five-star comments. All we needed was that first customer.

Ducking my head back into the call center, I saw Banderson on the phone AND texting at the same time. Wow! That was dedication. Unfortunately, after listening to him, it was clear he was talking to his mom about what was for dinner.

"*Noooo!* I HATE ravioli. Why can't you make meat loaf again? Okay . . . cool. No, I'm really bored!" said Banderson while he chatted with his mom and played Flappy Bird on his phone.

"Banderson! Who are you talking to?" I demanded.

"Sorry, Mom! Got to go . . . it's Buzz the Beekeeper. Love you, too!" said Banderson as he hung up. "Whaaat?!"

"Are you kidding? You called your mom about dinner?!" I asked.

"Big deal! You said I had to make twenty calls. I crushed that number. I've made twenty-six calls," answered Banderson.

"You're supposed to be calling people with pets! And trying to get them to hire Fur Cuttery," I said.

Apparently, everyone else followed Banderson's lead and just made random calls. Everyone except Naomi Sinclair, who suddenly shouted: "I GOT ONE!"

Jumping up and down, Naomi ran over to me (it all seemed to happen in slow motion, just so you know) and handed me a piece of paper.

"Jake. I did it! My neighbor has an old beagle named Oscar, and he wants

OSCAR →

us to wash him. Our first customer!" screamed Naomi.

Suddenly, Ms. Cane came stumbling through the curtain like a bull through a matador's cape.

"What?! Did we get one? Seriously! WA-HOOO!" bellowed Ms. Cane. "Thank goodness!"

She hugged Naomi and spun her around, and they both did a little dance. *Ah . . . excuse me, Ms. Cane, I'm pretty sure that's my job.*

Once Ms. Cane figured out where Naomi's neighbor lived, she hopped in the van and rocketed away from school. I'm surprised she didn't put a siren on top of the truck. What was the hurry? Oscar was still going to be dirty and smelly by the time she got there.

With Ms. Cane gone, the whole class relaxed. Work came to a grinding stop. DW III watched a movie on his iPad, Banderson called his mom back—he now wanted tacos instead of meat loaf—and Ajit started freestyling—which was never a good idea!

Yoooooo! MY name's Ajit,
and I'm the accounting Grandmaster,
Protecting Fur Cuttery cheese,
preventing financial disaster.
I handle all the cash, credit, and accounts receivable,
I also spit rhymes that are statistically unbelievable.

As I began to kick back and enjoy our first customer accomplishment, I got a text from Michael:

"MEETING NOW . . . MY OFFICE"

Ajit and Lesley received the same text, and within minutes all of us were sitting at Ms. Cane's desk while the rest of the class goofed off.

Sweet! Management meeting!

"I thought it important that we all meet. How's everything going? Anyone have any questions, problems? Is this thing going to work?" asked Michael.

"Dude, relax. This is definitely going to work!" I assured Michael.

"Are you sure, Jake?" asked Michael. "Are you sure everything is okay?"

"Yeah, cuz! I'm ready to count those dollars. But the cash river be dry like the Kalahari, yo!" yelled Ajit, turning his hat to the side acting all gangster.

Maybe this wasn't the brain-trust get-together I expected. It caught me off guard. Suddenly, I started to feel a little threatened by Michael's lack of confidence. Time to come out swinging.

"WAIT a minute! It's very easy for all of you to point fingers at me. I have the hardest job!" I insisted. "You think it's easy getting Banderson to do anything? And none of you have done anything to help. Oh, I'm sorry, Lesley, you did clean the brand-new truck.

- 127 -

That must have been really hard!" I yelled.

"And you. Mr. CE-YOOOO! What do you do all day? Besides text your new best bud, Jason. Look, we ALL know you made the A team, but that doesn't mean you're better than the rest of us. You have to work, too," I said.

WOW. That didn't come out right. Kind of wish I hadn't said that. #awkward

"Hey man, you asked to be Buzz Lightyear, not me. If it's too hard, then why don't you ask for help?" asked Michael, completely ignoring my lacrosse jealousy.

"The REALITY is it's tough finding people who want to have their pets groomed. We tried friends and family, but lots of them don't even have pets," I said.

"Okay. So, what we need to do is find a certain type of person who really wants and needs our services," said Lesley.

Ajit started jumping up and down. I wasn't sure if it was a new dance, if he had to go to the bathroom, or if he had something to say. Just then, he transformed back to the nerdy scholar we knew him to be.

"Precisely! Identifying a narrow target market is critical. Jake, your team can no longer be random in its calling. We need a certain group of people who love pets, are easy to contact, and who will appreciate a company run by kids," stated Ajit, as if he were some kind of supersmart college professor.

Rising to his feet, Michael smacked me in the arm. "Got it!" was all he said as he dropped down behind a computer.

Quickly logging into Facebook, he went to his . . . grandmother's page?

"Look. Check it out. She belongs to all these dog groups." Michael pointed at the screen.

Oh no! Michael was right . . . AGAIN! The perfect target market. They love pets, are always home and easy to contact. I don't know one who didn't love talking to kids.

Yes . . . the answer was old people! Grandma, Nana, Gramps, Bubbe, Mimi, Pop-Pop . . . you know, the people that get to boss your parents around. They were the answer.

How had I missed them? I was supposed to be the Facebook wizard? I was also supposed to be a lacrosse star? What was wrong with me? The only thing I could come up with was that Michael was somehow secretly stealing my AWESOMENESS. That had to be it!

But I had no time to worry about that, because staring back at me on the computer screen was the mother lode of pet-grooming opportunities. Tons of groups, and many of them local:

HOWARD COUNTY BARKS AND GEEZERS

GRAYS WITH GREYHOUNDS

RETIRED & RETRIEVING

OLD FOGIES AND YORKIES

SENIOR BOXERS ASSOCIATION

VETERANS BOWWOW

MARYLAND MATURES LOVE MUTTS

OLD FRIENDS, NEW DOGS

TIME-CHALLENGED TAIL-WAGGERS

And there weren't just a few members in each group. There were hundreds!

"YES! Perfect. Jake, this is all we need. What grandma is going to turn down a kid?" asked Lesley.

The answer was NONE. Not one. It was time to get to work.

CHAPTER 16
GOING APE

Great moments in history are easy to identify. Edison with the lightbulb. Caveman with the fire. Neil Armstrong walks on the moon. The day Fur Cuttery, Inc., figured out old people would buy anything from kids.

Think about it—where does the $50 million per year in Girl Scout Cookies sales come from? Grandmas and grandpas, of course!

Those shifty little sash-wearing marketing machines totally target the elderly. When Girl Scouts show up at my house and see me, their

I'LL PUT YOU DOWN FOR 1,000 BOXES?

smiles disappear and they walk away in disgust.

By stalking the elderly dog-and-cat Facebook groups, we soon were finding hundreds of potential customers every day. Before we knew it, Fur Cuttery, Inc., was rolling. Ms. Cane was in flea-and-tick heaven.

In no time, Ms. Cane turned from wicked stepsister to fairy godmother. With the money pouring in, she was all Hershey's Kisses and cookies. Seriously! She stocked the Beehive's shelves with whatever candy/treats we wanted.

Ms. Cane was smart, and she knew how to keep the worker bees buzzing. The twenty-call quota quickly became forty, and nobody complained. Candy . . . the breakfast of winners!

Soon enough, every kid wanted to be in the Hive. We were the rock stars of the company.

Ms. Cane never turned down a grooming opportunity— she'd even take multiple appointments at the same time. Once she had all the dogs collected, Ms. Cane would call Lesley on her cell and whip her truck into the back parking lot, where two or three of the Clean Team would be waiting. Within seconds, the kids were walking the pets into the building as Ms. Cane hit the gas and lit the tires. NASCAR teams had nothing on Lesley's well-coordinated "pet stop."

Lesley's team had washing tubs and special cutting/grooming tables, and the sound of blow dryers could be heard constantly. On some days, the hair on the floor was as deep as the hay in a barn.

The Clean Team got so fast at grooming, we usually had a bunch of dogs and cats just sitting there, probably wondering, WHY am I in an elementary school?

Of course, dogs and cats don't really like each other. Now put a whole bunch of them in a classroom filled with unsupervised sixth-graders. We had all the makings of a dog-cat-brawl disaster. But even the toughest dog or most vicious hissing cat was no match for Lesley the pet whisperer.

One wag of her tiny finger or one loud SHHHHH! from

her scrunched-up, annoyed face was all it took for Baxter and Mittens to be scared straight.

And if they didn't behave, it was off to doggie jail.

One afternoon, I walked through the Hive and saw Banderson on the phone. He was frantically motioning for me to come over.

"Of COURSE, Mrs. Larson. We are expert groomers. We love all pets!" assured Banderson as he made funny faces, mimicking the caller.

"A gibbon? Huh? Really? Why not?" said Banderson.

Waving my hands and mouthing NO, I tried to hang up the call. Banderson blocked my way.

"Yes! We've groomed hundreds, if not thousands of monkeys," lied Banderson. "Not a monkey? Oh, it's an ape.

No problem," assured Banderson.

"No, no, I get it. If I was a gibbon living in Maryland, I'd be a little unfriendly, too," said Banderson.

DON'T FORGET BEHIND THE EARS.

"We look forward to meeting you and Zeus tomorrow morning. Have a great day!" said Banderson as he hung up.

"*Yeaaaaahhh!* I DID it! I broke the record. Nine appointments confirmed in one day!" screamed Banderson. "Ms. Cane is going to freak out!"

"Do you think she'll freak out before or after she's mauled by an unfriendly Zeus?" I asked.

"Are you kidding? She's going to LOVE IT!" said Banderson. "Besides, what gibbon could possibly take Ms. Cane? Unless his name is King Kong, my money is on our pink-haired prison guard. Good luck, Zeus!"

There was a part of me that wanted to send that

appointment confirmation over to the Clean Team. Maybe Ms. Cane would love it? In the end, I had Banderson call back and cancel.

Fur Cuttery, Inc., was taking over pet grooming in Howard County. But we still had our limitations. The next day, a new sign went up at the entrance of the Beehive:

NO EXOTICS . . . ESPECIALLY APES!

CHAPTER 17
HELP WANTED

Meanwhile, Alexis was still going with the whole silent routine at dinner. Evidently, her FEAR game was a work in progress. I felt like an only child at times. All Mom and Dad did was focus on me. They loved hearing about all our crazy success at Fur Cuttery, Inc.

"Jake, I'm so proud of you," said Dad. "This is going to look great on your permanent record."

"Honey, he's in sixth grade. I don't think he has a 'record' just yet," said Mom.

"Sounds like you really love your job, Jake," said Alexis.

"WHOA! What was that?" I asked, pretending to be

shocked. "Did you guys hear someone talk?"

"Very funny. Maybe I'LL get a job at Fur Cuttery," said Alexis.

"Maybe NOT! We run a full background check on all employees. Sorry, no toilet-papering felons allowed," I said.

"Really. Doesn't say anything about that here in the ad," said Alexis as she pushed forward a colorful flier. I could see the Fur Cuttery logo all over it.

I snatched up the flier and read it quickly. How did I not know about this? Apparently, Ms. Cane was looking for middle-school kids to help out in the afternoon. She was offering service hours as credit.

"What's the matter, Jake? You mean Ms. Cane didn't share this with the Boss of Buzz?" asked Alexis. "I guess you're not that important, after all."

"Of course she did!" I said. (I was lying.) "Actually, it was Michael's idea. He told me about it."

"Sure he did. Oh yeah, I hear Michael has a new best friend. Mom, can you believe Michael is best buds with Jason from across the street?" asked Alexis.

"Really? Jake, you and Michael aren't friends anymore?" asked Mom.

"Of course we're friends. It's just that Michael needs to bond with his A team, and I totally get that," I said.

"And are you bonding with your fellow *Bee* teamers?" asked Alexis. "Maybe you guys can *buzz* around together."

Alexis was still raging over the whole no-sleepovers punishment—AND the fact that such lawless behavior got her kicked off her school's eighth-grade lacrosse team.

"You know what, Alexis? On second thought, I think working at FCI would be great for you. The Clean Team is complaining about all the hair and grossness they have to deal with," I explained.

DEAL WITH THIS.

"With Ms. Cane working late, the truck is a complete mess in the morning. Lesley and her team hate cleaning it. YOU could be the answer they are looking for!" I said.

"Don't even joke about that, Jake!" screamed Alexis. "You'd DO that for me? Seriously? O-M-G . . . you're the best brother ever! When do I start?"

Hmm? Not following. Waaaiiit a minute . . . I get it. More games from my crafty sister.

"Alexis, are you sure?" asked Mom. "Don't have Jake get you this job if you are not serious."

"MOM! I couldn't be more serious. It sounds incredible. And with Jake recommending me, I'm totally in," said Alexis, smiling at me.

Okay, big sister. You got it! She could fool Mom and Dad but not me. The next morning at work, I went directly to Michael's office.

"Dude, what's the deal with us hiring middle-schoolers?" I asked.

"Ms. Cane's idea. I had nothing to do with it. She told

me after she sent the fliers over," responded Michael.

"So who decides which middle-school kids to hire?" I asked.

"I guess that's me. And it goes to the first one stupid enough to want it," said Michael. "I don't think we'll get many interested kids."

"You might get one. Alexis wants to work here," I said.

"Oh man! Why?! I know she's your sister, but come on!" pleaded Michael. "Every time she sees me all she does is practice her new karate moves. Do you know what it's like to get hit by her?"

Yeah, I knew exactly what it was like—I had spent eleven years of living in fear of constant welts and bruises. I also knew Alexis hated to clean even more than she disliked sharing her Galactic Brownies. She'd be a no-show for sure.

CHAPTER 18
BETRAYAL

As Michael and I laughed about the thought of Alexis joining Fur Cuttery, Inc., Ms. Cane arrived looking extra grumpy.

"Bosses! My office. PRONTO!" screamed Ms. Cane.

As we all scrambled to find a place to sit, Ms. Cane cut right to the chase.

"I'm a little depressed after meeting with Grandmaster Cash over here," said Ms. Cane, pointing at Ajit.

"Really?! I thought everything was fine. You're getting seven to eight appointments a day," I said.

Ms. Cane just glared at me.

"That's not enough. Which brings me to why I called everyone in here," said Ms. Cane, pointing right at me. "Did YOU actually cancel one of my appointments last week? A Mrs. Larsen? Ring a bell?"

"Yeah. That's the lady with the gibbon, right?" I answered.

"Exactly. Where did you get the authority to cancel my appointments? Aren't you the Boss of Buzz? In charge of GETTING me appointments?" asked Ms. Cane.

"Yes?" I muttered. "But a gibbon? Isn't that a little dangerous?"

"Listen, Buzzy. Under NO circumstances are you to cancel anything. I don't care if it's a hyperactive baby T. REX, I'll groom it!" shouted Ms. Cane.

"Do you have ANY idea how much that hunk-of-junk truck cost me?" asked Ms. Cane.

I did not.

"The next time you decide to take money out of my pocket, Jake, get ready to join Mitch and DW moneybags on the cleaning crew," said Ms. Cane.

Oookay! Please . . . please . . . please let someone call in looking to have their newly adopted wolverine bathed and massaged.

"On the topic of making more money, I've been thinking a lot about how Fur Cuttery, Inc., can do just that," said Ajit.

Interested, Ms. Cane motioned for Ajit to continue.

"Lately, we've been brainstorming on how to make more money from each customer. You know, in addition to the basic cut, wash, and trim services."

"Is there a point to this?" interrupted Ms. Cane.

"I think my team and I have come up with some sweet new moneymaking ideas that I can show you on my iPad," said Ajit.

"I present to you, the future of FUR CUTTERY, INC.,"
announced Ajit. "Americans spend sixty-one billion per year
on their pets. We need to get more of that money."

"I like the sound of that, Grandmaster Cash! Tell me
more," pleaded Ms. Cane sarcastically.

"Okay. . . here we go.

"Idea number one—pet apparel: coats,
scarves, sweaters, shoes, sunglasses.

"Get it? Owners treat their dogs
like people. A high-end pet-clothing
company is what we need to do." Ajit
scanned the audience for reactions.
Nothing.

"Don't like that one? I have more!" assured Ajit.

"Idea number two—customized cuts. Owners like to
treat their dogs like people, so let's make them look like
people, too.

"I'm talking crazy dye jobs, colored pedicures,
dreadlocks, piercings, Mohawks . . . off-the-chain cuts and

customizations!" roared Ajit enthusiastically.

Again, silence.

"Okay. Forget that. You're going to love this next one. Ready?

"Idea number three: Parrot-Harmony—a dating service for parrots!

YOU MUST BE TIRED BECAUSE YOU'VE BEEN FLYING THROUGH MY HEAD ALL NIGHT.

EWW.

"Think about it. Parrots are one of the few species of birds that can mate for life. But they're not going to find the loves of their parrot lives sitting in cages. We set up a web-based dating site . . ."

Ms. Cane interupted. "Thank you, Ajit."

"Jake has done a great job getting us off the ground. But he doesn't have the creativity to take this company to the top," stated Ajit.

Hello! Did he just say that? Thanks a lot, Benedict Arnold. His betrayal was certainly not going to get Ajit any props from his work "homies."

"Ohhhhh, Ajit. So confused are we. Happy not counting money and paying bills, me think," said Ms. Cane. I made a mental note of her Yoda-AWESOMENESS.

Ms. Cane quickly explained to Ajit that he was irreplaceable as Grandmaster Cash.

That afternoon Ms. Cane arranged for the Queen of Clean to give Ajit a hands-on tutorial on proper de-fleaing techniques and toenail clipping. Ajit received Ms. Cane's message loud and clear.

CHAPTER 19
JELLY LUMBERJACK

Stepping out of the Hive, it was almost lunchtime. I was rumbly in my tumbly. Yeah! I still sometimes think in Winnie-the-Pooh terms. But only in my internal voice. You never know who's listening. People are so quick to judge nowadays.

But there's nothing wrong with Pooh Bear. That dude's legit, and I can definitely relate to him:

He's always hungry, doesn't like to wear pants, and is constantly looking over his shoulder out of fear of being bounced on by that psycho Tigger. Sound familiar?

Heading toward the door, I saw Michael standing next to his desk, so I went over to see if he was ready to eat. Surprisingly, he could still go to lunch like a regular student without being mauled by the lacrosse-loving student body. And yes, his head still fit between the lockers on either side of the hallway—barely.

"Can you believe MC Ajit? Nice sneak attack. Honestly, I didn't see that coming," I said.

"Well, this is business. At least he's competitive and going after what he wants one hundred percent," said Michael.

"What the does that mean?" I questioned.

"What do you mean, 'What does that mean?'" asked Michael.

"Sounds like you have something to say. What? I'm not competitive? I don't give one hundred percent?" I asked.

150

"Man, you're sensitive. Forget I said anything," said Michael.

"No, I wouldn't forget. Looks like the A team turned you into a real jerk. You know what your problem is, Mr. CE-YO?" I said, poking my finger in Michael's face.

But before I could explain exactly how I was feeling about my former best friend, the hairs on the back of my neck stood up. I felt instantly uneasy. There was an evil, unnatural presence at Fur Cuttery, Inc., What was happening?

"WHERE'S JAKEY?!" announced Alexis as she strolled into class. Tigger was in the building.

Since the middle school was next door, and they had half days on Wednesday, Alexis decided to stop by and introduce herself.

Spotting me from across the room, Alexis did the arm-extended, long-distance air hug and rushed forward. Like a mom scooping up her toddler from the pre-K sandbox, Alexis let out an embarrassing "THERE HE IS!" She immediately swung me off the ground in a bear-hug death grip.

Noticing Michael out of the corner of her eye, Alexis quickly released me and let out an equally fake-sounding "O-M-G!" and moved in for yet another suffocating embrace.

But the years of Tang Soo Do training paid off for Michael. Sidestepping Alexis's super squeeze, Michael was able to ninja roll over his desk and put distance between him and my big sister.

"Michael Boyd! What? No hug for me?" Alexis laughed, trying to pretend his reaction was perfectly normal. But the only thing that wasn't normal was Alexis. More specifically, what the heck was she wearing?

Alexis's naturally blond hair was now tinted a dark shade of purple. And she was wearing a baggy flannel shirt, black leggings, and giant black boots. Immediately it hit me—that was her Halloween costume from last year when she went as an emo lumberjack.

Of course, such an entrance attracted the attention of the entire class, not to mention Ms. Cane.

"Hello! And you are?" asked Ms. Cane.

"*ERMAHGERD!* Are you Ms. Cane?" blurted out Alexis, as if she just met the president or Edward the vampire guy. "Love your hair! ADORBS! I'm Alexis, Jake's sister. Jake! You never told me your teacher was so cool!"

"Oh my! Thank you, Alexis. Aren't you the sweetest thing!" said a blushing Ms. Cane.

"I am so sorry for interrupting your day. But when I found out you were looking for help, I had to run over," said Alexis. "I love animals so much. Here, I brought my résumé."

Résumé? What could it possible say? *Aerodynamic Associate—Toilet Paper Division*, or maybe it listed her advance degree in brotherly torment.

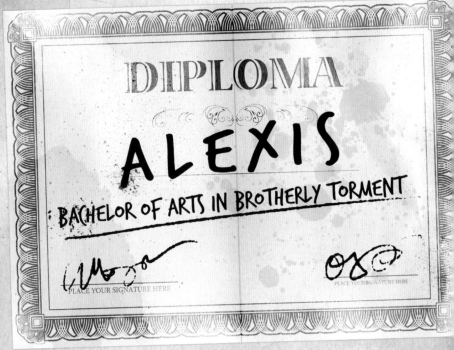

DIPLOMA

ALEXIS

BACHELOR OF ARTS IN BROTHERLY TORMENT

PLACE YOUR SIGNATURE HERE

PLACE YOUR SIGNATURE HERE

"No way!!!! Is that a BOXY!" screamed Alexis, pointing to Ms. Cane's picture of her pet turtle, Mr. Fred.

"Yup! Freddy is my baby! Just turned three last week," said a proud Ms. Cane.

"I'm totally jelly! I want one so bad, but this guy here is scared of most living creatures," said Alexis as she grabbed me in a playful headlock and tussled my hair.

"No kidding? That explains why he loves marketing so much. Scared of the customers!" Ms. Cane laughed.

"Totes McGoats!" Alexis said, laughing. "But seriously, I'm not scared of any animal and would love a chance to get knee deep in dog hair, fur, whatever you got."

The two of them kept laughing and continued their unusual bonding session while Ms. Cane gave Alexis the grand tour.

Suddenly, I lost my appetite. It felt like a tornado had ripped through Fur Cuttery, Inc., smashing my credibility like some flimsy corn silo. It took Alexis two minutes to destroy weeks of hard work and sucking up.

Ms. Cane acted like she was back in middle school and Alexis was her new BFFL.

That afternoon Alexis was officially the newest member of FCI. But there would be no fur sweeping or drool mopping in Alexis's immediate future.

Of course not, silly! You don't let your bestie start at the bottom and work her way up. Instead, if you're Ms. Cane, you announce to the class that my big sister is the new Overlord of Customer Care.

In a move that left the entire class in shock, the two new best buddies drove off to the afternoon appointments giggling and talking about iced coffee and celebrity gossip. I'm sure they made time for a Forever 21 and Starbucks run. YOLO!

The only person more upset than me about our new Overlord of Customer Care was Lesley. She was supposed to be the Queen of Clean. Was Alexis her new boss?

CHAPTER 20
YOU'RE FIRED

That night I decided to order room service. Faking a headache and lying in bed, I couldn't stomach the thought of sitting at the same table with Alexis.

I was the one who ripped out the soul of her eighth-grade existence. And now it was time for payback.

If she was willing to abandon her unofficial uniform of straight blond hair, Lululemon headbands, Abercrombie shirts, and Hollister jeans for a depressed-lumberjack look, I was in BIG trouble.

That week, Ms. Cane called a company meeting. It was the first time she spoke to us as a class since launching Fur

Cuttery, Inc. Most kids expected a party to celebrate our five hundredth customer. Ms. Cane had other plans.

Instead of cake and pats on the back, we got a lecture on our laziness. Ms. Cane stood in front of us and demanded we give "one hundred ten percent every day" and challenged everyone at Fur Cuttery, Inc., to be committed to the "pursuit of excellence."

As soon are we heard those words, Michael and I looked at each other in horror. That was Alexis talking. Actually, both those phrases are on giant posters in her basement weight room. She was brainwashing Ms. Cane.

How easily Ms. Cane forgot all our planning, effort, and hard work. A bunch of sixth-graders launched her business and within weeks filled her appointment book with hundreds of customers. We were the biggest thing in the grooming industry since No Tears Ringworm Rinse.

All that didn't matter. Ms. Cane wanted MORE! She also explained that none of our positions were "jobs for life" and big changes could be coming if she didn't see improvement. So much for hard work and creating my own luck. Was working for a company just like school—one big popularity contest? *Nooooooo!!!!!!!!!*

Within days of coming aboard, everyone at Fur Cuttery, Inc., lived in fear of our new overlord. She was Ms. Cane's eyes and ears, and nobody escaped her critical eye. Basically, Alexis was the company bully.

She acted like a test monitor, slowly walking around the class, on the lookout for slackers and anyone goofing off. She enjoyed making everyone uncomfortable. I'd never really seen her smile before.

I felt the worst for Lesley. Because with the new OC up on the wall, there were no more questions about who was in charge of pet operations. The Overlord controlled everything to do with pets, grooming, and appointments, and Lesley was number two.

Although it was rare for Alexis to lower herself and actually speak to sixth-graders, she always found time to share words of encouragement with Lesley:

"Geez Louise. Not so deep into her ear channel with that cotton swab. You're not mining for gold!"

"No . . . no . . . NO!!! We don't muzzle. EVER! How long have you been here?"

"Lesley! Just listen to me. The quieter you become, the more you can hear!"

"Haven't you heard of aromatherapy? What kind of operation you running here? *Lavender*, Lesley, LA. VEN. DER!"

That Friday turned out to be doomsday. Ms. Cane was in earlier than usual and TAKE A SEAT was written on the board in big, bold letters. I knew what was coming. It was about to get ugly!

"Apparently, some of you aren't taking the business seriously. I guess my warnings weren't enough. So, with that said, I'm making some changes," announced Ms. Cane.

Lesley, her arms firmly crossed, started to breathe heavy. I didn't think she was the hyperventilating type.

But waiting to be fired must be awful. It was all so embarrassing—so public!

Ms. Cane started off by announcing a few lower-level moves. AJ Fish was moved to the Hive, and Lauren Giles was going to accounting. Then came the BIG STUFF.

"Okay! Regarding management—there is one significant change. Although I do appreciate everyone's hard work up to this point, I need to make this move in order to take Fur Cuttery, Inc., to the NEXT LEVEL," said Ms. Cane. *Hmm? Another Alexis phrase. Too funny!*

"Starting today, DW III is the new Boss of Buzz. Jake will be taking DW III's old position in operations," announced Ms. Cane.

At first, I thought there was some kind of mistake.

"Me?! I'm going to the truck? What did I do?" I asked, trying desperately not to overreact. You never know, this could be some kind of test or something.

"That's correct. Sorry. Like I said, I had to make a change," said Ms. Cane as she walked back to her desk. "All

- 161 -

right. The show's over, let's get to work. We have lots to do."

But nobody moved. Everyone was in shock. I got up and walked to the front of the room, I wasn't going down without a fight.

"That's crazy. I'm doing a great job! Why are you doing this? You fired me for nothing," I said.

"Jake, you haven't been fired, just reassigned. It's no big deal. We only have a few weeks left, anyway. It's time to give someone else a chance," said Ms. Cane.

"It's no big deal to you, maybe. But it's a very big deal to me. I've been working my butt off for you. We get you eight to ten appointments every day," I said as calmly as possible, trying hard to change her mind.

"Jake, I know you're passionate about your work, but the decision is final. I need to do what's best for Fur Cuttery, Inc.," said Ms. Cane. "I hope you understand."

"No. I DON'T. But I hope you UNDERSTAND I need to do what I need to do," I said.

Standing in front of my teacher, I was shaking mad. Then I noticed Michael approaching.

"Come on, Ms. Cane, this is bull. Fur Cuttery, Inc., is blowing up because of Jake's work. I don't get it. Why?" asked Michael.

"Listen CE-YO, I don't need to explain myself," said Ms. Cane. "Just be happy it wasn't you. Unless, of course, you'd like to join your pal on the cleaning crew?"

"This company is a joke. I'd rather be covered in dog hair and fur balls than work another second as your CE-anything. I'm done. Come on, Jake, let's get cleaning," said Michael.

"Ms. Cane, it's foolish to lift a rock only to drop it on your foot," Michael said to Ms. Cane.

"Wow. How worldly. Now, go get some cleaning supplies and a mop. And make sure not to drop those on YOUR foot," Ms. Cane said with a laugh.

Lesley quickly escorted us out. While changing into my hazmat suit and putting on the required rubber gloves, reality finally hit me. No wonder everyone hated being in operations. It was disgusting!

"Hey, Michael . . . thanks, man. But you didn't have to do that," I said.

"Sure I did. That's what best friends do," said Michael as he adjusted his chemical-splash-proof goggles.

"Does this mean you're quitting the A team, too?" I asked, half kidding.

"Not a chance." Michael laughed.

CHAPTER 21
BLACK EYE

Ms. Cane might have just won that battle, but she started a war with the wrong kid.

In my world of AWESOMENESS, I don't simply accept unjust situations. I fight hard against them like a zombie-apocalypse survivalist. Nobody's going to eat my brains!

So, with no other alternative, I decided to do what I do best: Get even. Ms. Cane was about to find out that if you push too many kids around on the playground, sooner or later one of them is going to give you a black eye.

Michael and I made it through the morning, barely. At lunchtime, we stepped out of our protective coveralls and raced to the library for a top secret strategy meeting.

With Ms. Cane out on grooming appointments the rest of the day, the former Boss of Buzz and former CE-YO of Fur Cuttery, Inc., agreed it was time to blow up the Death Star. And there was only one way to do it.

THAT'S NO MOON! IT'S A SPACE STATION!

CHILL, DUDE. IT'S A MOON.

Michael took to Twitter and Yelp, and I was responsible for wrecking FCI's credibility on Facebook and Angie's List. Soon, social media would be flooded with awful reports and "customer" complaints about the company we both helped build.

@FurCuttery Please NEVER call me again. Your prices are insanely high, and your customer service is RUDE and completely unprofessional.

@FurCuttery You should be ashamed of yourselves, my dog's haircut was TERRIBLE. Talk about amateur hour. I want my $ back! #yourefired

Hired @furcuttery, to bathe Whiskers this morning. You can imagine my horror when THIS groomer showed up at my door. I called the police!

Best 90th BD ever . . . UNTIL @FurCuttery screwed up Mr. Rocky's 10:00 a.m. appointment. Then they yelled at me when I asked for a refund!

Walking out of school that afternoon, we were both confident Fur Cuttery, Inc., was doomed. Soon, Ms. Cane would be the crazy clown of the grooming world.

I still didn't know why she fired me. And that REALLY bugged me. On the bus ride home I kept thinking about possible reasons, but none made sense. I had to find out.

Could it be Alexis's mind-trick manipulation? Or was it Ms. Cane herself . . . overcome by her hatred of my AWESOMENESS? Or a combination of both?

My best shot at finding the truth would be that night at home.

— — — — — — — — — — —

I got to the dinner table a few minutes early to secure the best seat. Mom was just coming in from work, and Dad was feverishly laying out the trimmings for his world-famous tacos. He used bison meat, which was an Alexis favorite. She was obsessed with lean proteins and building muscle mass.

Not telling anyone about my "reassignment," I kept my parents busy with predinner small talk. Seeing Alexis's first reaction to me talking calmly was critical. She'd expect to see me complaining and ranting, and her facial expression would give her away.

With the aroma of fried bison wafting through the house, Alexis could hardly contain her excitement. I heard her bounding down the stairs.

"OH YEEAHH! Grass-fed goodness!" shouted Alexis.

Barreling into the kitchen, her first stop was the stove. After quickly shoving a spoonful of bison meat into her mouth, Alexis walked into the dining room. Immediately, she lit up like a Christmas tree.

"Boo-YAH! There he is! My little broom boy!" screamed Alexis, spitting out meat all over the table.

"Alexis! Please. Cover your mouth. You are a lady!" shrieked Mom.

"Mom! Don't go anywhere. You have to hear this!" laughed Alexis. "Dad! Where's Dad? Get in here! You are not going to believe what happened. Jake got some AWESOME real-world experience today at school!"

"What's the big deal? Is Jake the new CEO?" asked Dad, crossing his fingers in anticipation.

"Yeah right! Not quite!" cackled my big sister.

"What's she talking about, Jake?" asked Mom.

"Go ahead, Jakey, break their little hearts!" insisted Alexis.

As I explained what happened, seeing my parents' disappointed faces fueled my inner rage.

"She didn't give you any reason?" asked Mom. "She just fired you?"

"Ms. Cane said something about kids not taking the business seriously. And some junk about 'committing one hundred ten percent' and the 'pursuit of excellence,'" I said as I turned to stare at my sister.

"Yeah! That's NEXT LEVEL stuff right there! Pump them up, Ms. Cane-O! Love it!" yelled Alexis.

"Alexis. You spend a lot of time with Ms. Cane. Did she say anything to you about Jake?" asked Dad.

"Me?" asked Alexis, quickly changing her tone to a higher-pitched, innocent voice of disbelief.

"Yes, YOU! Do you know why Jake was fired?" asked Dad again.

"Hold on. I had nothing to do with it," insisted Alexis. "Don't blame me. He's an annoying know-it-all, and I'm sure everyone is sick of his nonstop—"

My dad raised his hand in the air and motioned for her to stop. Being on her best behavior and hoping to someday get another shot at sleepovers, Alexis shut it down.

"I'm not blaming you. All I'm asking is whether you know why?" asked Dad directly.

"I don't know exactly why. All I know is Ms. Cane has been spending a lot of time meeting with the dad of that little dork who carries the briefcase," said Alexis.

Aha! It was DW III. I wonder why Ms. Cane was meeting with Mr. Winston?

Grabbing two tacos and heaping lump of refried beans, I excused myself. Sniffling and faking tears, I told my mom I needed to be alone. Of course she understood.

Soon enough, thanks to my good pals Google and Bing, I found out everything there was to know about DW III's dad, Mr. Winston. Apparently, that guy was really rich. He made kazillions by starting Internet companies back in the nineties. Nowadays he liked to help entrepreneurs grow their businesses.

I wonder how much it cost to buy DW III's freedom from the cleaning crew? Whatever the amount, it was a bad investment.

CHAPTER 22
CYBORG MAKEOVER

We didn't think there would be an overnight victory in our war against Ms. Cane. So Michael and I sucked it up as best we could for the rest of the week. Morning cleanups were the worst. It was like swimming in a sea of fur and disgustingness.

Our relief came in the form of a long holiday weekend. With no school on Monday, we doubled our attack on FCI with even more awful reviews, crazy posts, and outrageous tweets. Our cyber offensive was raging, and I was certain Ms. Cane had no idea what was happening.

Walking into school Tuesday morning, I looked forward

to seeing Ms. Cane slumped over her desk and weeping uncontrollably. DW III would be holding a box of tissues and offering tender "there, there"s. Or, better yet, our class would be a scene of out-of-control chaos, with a crazed Ms. Cane chasing DW III around the room with a broom. *That's right, smush him like a bug, Ms. C.!*

Super psyched, I walked even faster down the hall. I hoped I hadn't missed any of the WWE-style action.

Unfortunately, there was no sweet revenge that morning. Everything looked heartbreakingly normal.

Three steps into class, Lesley was all over me to get the truck ready. Ms. Cane had a 9:00 a.m. wash, trim, and clip, and she didn't want to be late. *Huh?!*

Looking over at Lesley's dry-erase board, the day was packed with appointments. We were actually busier than normal. We hadn't put a dent into the Fur Cuttery, Inc., moneymaking machine.

My AWESOMENESS was directly responsible for creating an indestructible alien cyborg business that was now controlled by the evil Ms. Cane. And she grew stronger by the day.

After hours of stuffing green garbage bags full of mildewy pet cuttings, Michael and I needed fresh air and nourishment. Depressed and exhausted, we stumbled into the cafeteria. I was never happier to smell our school's highly questionable cheeseburger, macaroni, and taco platter.

"I can't take this much longer," said Michael as we sat down together at lunch. "I stink of dog, and even after I shower I still smell like a kennel."

Throwing her brown-bagged lunch down on the table, Lesley Kim joined us looking equally depressed.

"I know what you guys are doing," said Lesley.

"What are you talking about?" I asked.

"Really? You don't think I watch what's going on online? Twitter? Facebook? All the ridiculous reviews? It can only be you two morons," said Lesley.

"They don't sound real to you?" asked Michael.

"*Duuude!* What are you doing?" I said, shaking my head at Michael and wishing he'd shut his mouth.

"Don't worry, Jake. Your secret cyber assault is safe with me. I won't tell anyone," assured Lesley. "But it will never work. The old people love us."

DW III interrupted our conversation. "Lesley! What ARE you doing? You're the Queen of Clean—the boss of operations! Act like it! You don't sit and eat with the help." DW III laughed. "Now come on and join me over at the management table."

"Management? That's hilarious. If your daddy has to pay for you to be on the management team, are you really management?" I asked.

"You're such a funny guy, Jake. I could listen to your jokes all day. But I can't, because in about ten minutes you have to go mop out the truck and sterilize some clippers. Good times!" said DW III.

As DW III sauntered away, Lesley leaned in close to me and Michael. She looked intense.

"Listen, what I'm about to tell you is HUGE! Tomorrow, we're doing a group groom for the Westminster White Hairs with Westies. There are ten dogs, and each is getting the head-to-paw treatment," said Lesley. "The leader of the group, Mr. Jefferies, loves to talk to Ms. Cane, so I know Alexis will be alone in the truck grooming by herself."

HEAD-TO-PAW NAY, METHINK NOT.

"So? Why is that 'HUGE'?!" I asked, still completely confused by whispering Lesley.

"It's important because Mr. Jefferies is a FREAK about his precious Sir Lancelot's appearance," said Lesley. "That dog is famous. He's the cute little white dog you see in all the Cesar dog food commercials."

"You lost me, Lesley," I said. "What does that have to do with us?"

"Well, if you two really want to destroy FCI, you'll be interested to know that when Alexis is grooming, she follows the client instructions exactly as they appear on the appointment ticket," explained Lesley, frantically looking around as she spoke. "Basically, Alexis will groom a dog any way the confirmation ticket tells her to. And when I say any way, I mean *AN-Y-WAY*," said a giddy Lesley.

A wide-eyed Michael sat straight up, crossed his arms, and started grinning ear to ear.

"You didn't lose me," said Michael, leaning across the table and high-fiving the Queen of Clean. "And you still email the appointment tickets to Alexis?"

"YES, I do. And come to think of it, my computer is on right now with my email account WIDE open. Silly me!" said Lesley. "Can you guys do me a HUGE favor and go close my email for me. I was just about to fill out tomorrow's grooming instructions for Sir Lancelot."

AHA! Finally, I understood.

"I just can't take Alexis anymore," said Lesley. "I think it's time for Sir Lancelot's makeover. Perfect snow-white fur is so BORING. I heard he really wants to look like Ms. Cane."

"What a coincidence, I heard the same thing."

CHAPTER 23
THE BIG
REVEAL

Like I always say, *Go big, or go home!* With regards to Sir Lancelot's new appointment ticket we emailed to Alexis . . . we went beyond BIG.

If everything went according to plan, the Westminster White Hairs with Westies would soon be looking for a new mobile pet groomer.

But since the Westie group groom wasn't until early afternoon, I'd have to wait until Alexis got home that night to see if Sir Lancelot liked his new "custom" look.

Michael and I didn't talk much on the bus ride home that day. We especially didn't talk about you-know-what.

Too risky. You never knew who's listening. When my stop came, I grabbed my backpack, fist-bumped Michael, and said I'd text him later.

Turning into my driveway, I suddenly heard the faint rumble of a diesel-powered engine. In the distance, I could see a van approaching, going WAY too fast for my neighborhood.

In an instant, I recognized the all-too-familiar paw logo and the crazy pink-haired driver behind the wheel.

Slamming on the brakes in front of my house, the van's side door quickly swung open and Alexis leaped to the safety of our front lawn. Gunning the engine, Ms. Cane took off, not even bothering to check if Alexis had closed the door. She hadn't.

DRAMATIC REENACTMENT

www.furcuttery.com

Fur Cutters INC.

ttery.com

Within seconds of Ms. Cane turning left at the top of my street—with a whole bunch of grooming supplies flying out of the side—another truck flew by us in hot pursuit. It had one of those satellite dishes on the roof and ACTION NEWS painted on the side.

Still laughing hysterically, Alexis finally calmed down enough to tell me the whole story. As it turned out, Sir Lancelot did indeed get his makeover. But it wasn't Alexis who gave it to him.

Evidently, the Westie grooming thing was a giant doggie party in celebration of Sir Lancelot's new commercial. Mr. Jefferies invited all his Westie owner buddies, their dogs, AND a local TV station to cover the event. In Westminster, Sir Lancelot was pretty big deal.

But as soon as Ms. Cane saw the reporters and cameramen, she tried to make the whole thing about her and Fur Cuttery, Inc. Kicking Alexis out of the van, Ms. Cane insisted on grooming Sir Lancelot herself and promised the crowd a new-and-improved superstar.

After about thirty minutes locked inside the grooming van, Ms. Cane texted Alexis and instructed her to gather the whole party around the van for Sir Lancelot's big reveal.

With cameras rolling, Ms. Cane triumphantly threw

open the door and marched out carrying Sir Lancelot high above her head just like that crazy baboon Rafiki held Simba in *The Lion King*.

Maybe the pressure of the situation fried her brain, but for whatever reason, Ms. Cane followed our fake grooming appointment ticket right down to the neon-green nail polish.

After the partygoers let out a collective GASP and after they called paramedics to revive Mr. Jefferies, a local TV reporter started getting into Ms. Cane's face and asking LOTS of questions.

Alexis couldn't remember if any punches were thrown, but she said they barely escaped the angry crowd.

— — — — — — — — — —

Not until after dinner, when we all sat down and watched the local news, did everyone get a better understanding of exactly what went down.

"Coming up next, a Channel Nine exclusive—SEVERE groomer misconduct leaves a local canine celebrity vandalized and his owner looking for answers. We have the shocking video! Stay tuned!"

O . . . M . . . G!!!

My dad didn't say anything. Calmly reaching for the remote, he pushed the RECORD button. Mom kept repeating, "Oh, I'm sure it's not THAT bad." But unfortunately for Ms. Cane . . . it was.

Yes, the outrageous grooming job she did on Sir Lancelot was damaging. And yes, the high-definition close-up of a weeping and fainting Mr. Jefferies didn't help matters, either. But, in the end, it was Ms. Cane's winning personality that was the star of the show.

HEATED EXCHANGE BETWEEN MS. CANE AND TV REPORTER:

Reporter: Who are you and what did you do to Sir Lancelot?

Ms. Cane: My name is Annabel Cane, owner of Fur Cuttery, Inc. At FCI, your paws are our pleasure.

Reporter: Really! Then why is everyone here so upset

by what you did to Sir Lancelot? You know the owner is crying? I believe they are calling the police as we speak?

Ms. Cane: Crying? They must be tears of joy! Just look at that little rascal. He's a freakin' rock star. That's how we roll at Fur Cuttery, Inc.

Reporter: You might be rollin' into a lawsuit real soon.

Ms. Cane: ~*grabbling the microphone*~ Look, buddy, I don't go to your job and tell you how to look pretty in front of a camera. So don't you tell me how to groom my clients. That's a customized cut, and you'll only find that at Fur Cuttery, Inc.

~*The reporter and Ms. Cane struggle over the mic and eventually fall to the ground. Chaos ensues with Ms. Cane running and leaping into her van and speeding away.*~

"Oh my!" said Dad, turning off the TV. "Kids, after what I just saw I think it's best if the both of you have no further contact with Ms. Cane or anything to do with Fur Cuttery, Inc."

"Really? How am I going to do that? She's my teacher. I'll see her tomorrow morning. Should I skip school?" I asked.

"I think you'll be okay, Jake. Something tells me you're going to have a substitute tomorrow," said Mom.

I'm sure Mom already had an update from BFF Principal McCracken.

With my parents in the other room, Alexis jumped out of her seat and threw me down on the couch. Pinning me with her knees on my shoulders, Alexis lowered her face inches away from mine.

"You and your stupid friend thought you could trick me into turning Sir Lancelot into some freak dog?" accused Alexis.

"No! What are talking about? *Ow!* Get off me, you fat load!" I pleaded.

"Truth time, Jakey. It had to be you. Lesley doesn't have the guts to do it herself. That only leaves you and Wild Boy," said Alexis. "And since both of you are now hair janitors, I'm positive you worked together."

"Okay . . . okay . . . it was us. So what?" I said.

"Do you really think I'm that stupid?" asked Alexis.

"I was kind of hoping you were," I said.

With that, Alexis dug her knees deeper into my shoulders.

"WHOOAA! Come on, get off!" I pleaded.

Letting me go and rolling onto the floor, Alexis looked happy. I had to ask the obvious question.

"But if you knew it was fake, why didn't you stop Ms. Cane?" I asked.

"Because she deserved it. Nobody bullies my little brother. That's my job," said Alexis.

It felt good to be loved!

CHAPTER 24
PREPARED
STATEMENTS

Our last week of school flew by. Everyone forgot about FCI, grooming, and making money. It was glorious.

On the morning of the last day, Principal McCracken was standing front and center in our classroom. Huh? What was this all about?

"Good morning, students," she said. "Please, everyone, take your seats. I realize this year has been, how should I say, *interesting*, but I want to take this time to clear up any rumors you might be hearing.

"First, I am delighted to tell everyone that Sir Lancelot is doing fine.

"Second, Mr. Jefferies is not pressing charges against FCI, Ms. Cane, or Kinney Elementary. Anything you hear about anyone going to prison is simply not true.

"Lastly, as of today, Ms. Cane is officially retired from teaching. However, I did want to bring her back this morning, because I think it's only fair she be given an opportunity to speak to you all and say good-bye. Annabel, come on in," said Principal McCracken, motioning toward the door.

Ms. Cane strutted in like she didn't have a care in the world. Her hair was pinker than usual, and it even looked like she'd been working out. Obviously, she enjoyed being known around the globe as the crazy groomer.

Reaching into her pocket, Ms. Cane pulled out a piece of paper and began to read. *Oh gosh, a prepared statement. What happened to the art of public speaking!*

"I want to thank all of you for your hard work and dedication. Working with you guys has been a life-changing experience for me. I will never forget any of you kids, and I hope everyone was able to learn from what we accomplished in this class.

"As for me, today I leave for California to start the next chapter in my life. Why? Because you guys are looking at the brand-new star of *Groomers Gone Wild*!

"Yup, I know: crazy, right! I got my own reality-TV show on the Truest TV Network. We go into production next week and will air next fall, Tuesday nights, after *Pampered Pageant Princess from Piscataway*.

"Thanks again, everyone. I'm terrible at good-byes. Make sure to watch my show. Oh yeah, before I forget, you'll find a little thank-you from me inside your desks. See ya, and have a great summer!"

Ajit was the first to open his desk. "WHAT THE . . . a MacBook Pro with a solar-powered charger. Are you KIDDING me!" screamed Ajit.

As I worked to open my box, I soon discovered a smaller box. Than another, and another, and another, until I got down to one the size of a small shoe box. It had some nice weight to it, so I knew it was still something of substance.

Ms. Cane was a funny lady. I guess in the end she really did appreciate my Boss of Buzz AWESOMENESS after all.

Lifting the lid on the last box, I slowly unwrapped the tissue paper and discovered Ms. Cane's Question Rock hiding inside. There was no note.

All around me I could hear the sweet music of MacBooks firing up as I continued to stare down at my new doorstop.

Sitting at my desk and tossing the rock up in air, I immediately thought about running out to the parking lot and throwing it through the grooming van's windshield. But that would make me no better than Ms. Cane. And if I was anything, I was better than that lady.

My mission was ultimate victory, which could take years to achieve. And yes, Ms. Cane, I will be watching your new show in the fall. But unfortunately for you, I have a feeling the online reviews for *Groomers Gone Wild* won't be very good.

ABOUT THE AWESOME AUTHOR

Jake Marcionette is an eighth-grader living with his mom, dad, and big sister in Florida. He wrote the manuscript for *Just Jake* when he was just twelve years old. His first book debuted at #7 on the *New York Times* Best Seller List. In addition to writing, Jake loves playing lacrosse and annoying his sister, Alexis. You can learn more about Jake at www.justjake.com.